BOOKS BY
ROBERT B. PARKER

AVAILABLE FROM DELL

Robert B. Parker

THE WIDENING GYRE

A Spenser Novel

A DELL BOOK

Published by
Dell Publishing
a division of
Random House, Inc.
New York, New York

ISBN: 978-0-440-19535-1

Reprinted by arrangement with Delacorte Press/Seymour Lawrence

Printed in the United States of America

One Previous Edition

December 1987

30 29 28 27 26 25 24 23

OPM

For Joan, David, and Daniel.
The center can hold, and does.

Turning and turning in the widening gyre
The falcon cannot hear the falconer;
Things fall apart; the center cannot hold; . . .

William Butler Yeats,
"The Second Coming"

Chapter 1

I was nursing a bottle of Murphy's Irish Whiskey, drinking it from the neck of the bottle sparingly, and looking down from the window of my office at Berkeley Street where it crosses Boylston.

It was dark and there wasn't much traffic down there. Across the street there were people working late in the ad agency, but the office where the brunette art director worked was dark. The silence in my office was linear and dwindling, like an art-perspective exercise. The building was pretty much empty for the night and the occasional faraway drone and jolt of the elevator only added energy to the silence.

I sipped a little whiskey.

When you thought about it, silence was rarely silent. Silence was the small noises you heard when the larger noises disappeared.

I sipped another small swallow of whiskey. The whiskey added a little charge to the silence. Irish whiskey was in fact excellent for thinking about things like silence.

A car came slowly down Berkeley Street and parked up on the curb below my office window by a sign that said TOW ZONE NO PARKING ANYTIME. A bulky man with a large red nose got out. I knew who he was.

Across Boylston Street, on the Bonwit's corner, a man and woman stood arms around each other waiting for the light to change so they could cross Berkeley. She had her left hand in his hip pocket. He had his arm over her shoulders. Was it love or was she lifting his wallet? The light changed. They crossed. Her hand still in his hip pocket. Love.

Behind me I heard the office door open. I turned away from the window and there was the bulky man with the red nose.

He said, "You Spenser?"

I said, "Yeah."

He said, "You know who I am?"

"Fix Farrell," I said.

"F.X." he said, "I don't like that nickname."

I said, "You want a slug of Murphy's Irish Whiskey?"

"Sure."

I handed him the bottle. He wiped the neck off automatically with the palm of his hand and took a slug. Then he handed me back the bottle.

"You a lush?" he said.

"No."

"I can't do business with no lush."

"Wouldn't that depend on the business?" I said.

Farrell shook his head. "Never mind that shit," he said. "I woulda heard if you was a lush."

I had a little more whiskey and offered him the bottle.

2 ——

He took it and drank some more. He had on a light gray overcoat with black velvet lapels and he was wearing a homburg. The hair that showed around the hat was gray. The shirt that showed above the lapels of the overcoat was white, with a pin collar and a rep stripe tie tied in a big windsor knot.

"I had you checked out, Spenser. You unnerstand? I had my people look into you pretty thorough, and you come out clean."

"Yippee," I said.

"We're going to hire you."

He gave me back the bottle. What made his nose red was a fine network of broken veins.

"The city council?" I said.

He shook his head impatiently. "No, for crissake, the Alexander campaign committee. We want you to handle security for us."

"Meade Alexander? The congressman?"

"Yeah. They told me you were smart as a whip. Meade's running for the Senate, or don't you read the papers?"

"Only the funny stuff," I said. "Tank MacNamara, and the City Council proceedings."

I drank a little more whiskey.

"Sure, sure," Farrell said, "you want the job?"

"Security," I said.

"Security. We've had some death threats and they're probably some left wing crackpot, but Browne's connected, so you gotta pay some attention."

"Browne? Alexander's opponent?"

"Yeah, Robert Browne."

"He's got mob affiliation?"

"Oh, yeah, sure." Farrell said. "Been in the bag for years."

"And you think the mob's trying to put a hit on Alexander?"

Farrell shook his head. "No. But you can't be sure, and we gotta have somebody to handle security anyway. Every campaign has to have security. Why not get the best."

"A gentleman of discerning sensibility," I said.

"Yeah, sure. You want the job?"

"Who's doing it now?"

"Couple of Fitchburg cops on temporary duty to the campaign staff. They'll stay, but you'd be in charge."

"Alexander's from Fitchburg?"

"Yeah."

"What mob has Browne in its pocket?" I said.

Farrell shrugged. "Who knows?"

"If you don't know who bought him, how do you know he's bought?" I said.

Farrell took the bottle from me again without asking and drank. Then he passed it back. I drank a much smaller swallow than he had.

"What the fuck are you, the editor of *The Boston Globe*? It doesn't matter what I can prove. We're talking politics, asshole."

"You don't know me well enough to call me pet names, Fix."

Farrell paid no attention. He looked at his watch.

"What d'ya say. You want the job or no? Money's not a sweat. We can get together on the money."

I turned away from Farrell briefly and stared out my window at the dark street and the darkened window of the art director and listened to the sounds of my office. Did I have something better to do? I did not. Could I use the money? Yes. Would it kill time for me better than drinking Irish whiskey and looking out the window? Maybe.

"You have any trouble with Alexander's politics?" Farrell asked my back.

I turned. "I have trouble with everybody's politics," I said.

"So what's the problem?" Farrell said.

"No problem," I said. "I'll take the job."

Chapter 2

Meade and Ronni Alexander were holding hands when I met them. He was tall and sort of rural looking with a good tan. His gray-blond hair was combed straight back. He wore a dark blue three-piece suit of miraculous fiber, a maroon tie with tiny figures, and black boots that closed with a zipper up the side.

His wife was smaller, with long blond hair styled the way Farrah Fawcett used to wear hers. She had very large blue eyes, long eyelashes, a wide mouth, and a small straight nose. Around her neck she wore a black velvet ribbon with a cameo brooch in front. Her blouse was white, pleated, and lacy at collar and cuffs. Her skirt was black; her shoes had very high heels. She smelled of good perfume and looked twenty years younger than her husband. She wasn't. He was fifty-one. She was forty-six.

We were in their suite at the Sheraton-Boston along with Fix Farrell and the two Fitchburg cops and a guy named Abel Westin, who was Alexander's media consultant. We all sat down, except Ronni, who got coffee from the room service wagon and began to serve it. I was speculating whether when she wrote her name she dotted the *i* with a little heart. I thought it was likely.

Alexander accepted a cup of coffee from his wife and said to me, "Are you a religious man, Mr. Spenser?"

"No."

"Were you raised in a Christian faith?"

"My people are Irish. I was raised Catholic."

"But you no longer believe."

"Nope."

"Do you believe in almighty God?"

"Why, does he want to hire me?"

Alexander sat back so abruptly that he spilled some coffee.

"Or she," I said.

Ronni Alexander got a napkin from the room service table and dabbed at her husband's trouser leg and at the rug, tucking her skirt carefully under her as she crouched. Alexander patted her shoulder.

"Thank you, Ronni," he said, still looking at me speculatively. "Mr. Spenser, whatever stereotype you have of politicians will not suitably characterize me. I am a Christian. It is the most important thing about me. I believe absolutely in a set of very clear imperatives. I will not at this time debate those imperatives with you. But do not take them lightly. It is in the service of Christ that I run for office, in the interest of implementing those imperatives. This country is desolate and needs to be redeemed."

I looked at Fix Farrell standing by the window with his hat on. His face remained impassive. Alexander continued.

"I do not require that you be a Christian. But I do require that you understand my faith and its power. We will be together often and sometimes continuously for some time. My wife and I are in earnest."

Farrell said, "Okay, Meade, cut the shit. We ain't hiring him to pray for you."

"Please be careful of your language, Francis, in front of Mrs. Alexander."

"Yeah, sure," Farrell said. "But Spenser is what we need in this job. My people checked him out real thorough. Yeah, he's a royal pain in the ass; but he's got the stuff. So let's get to it and stop frigging around."

Alexander smiled and shook his head slightly. He looked at me a moment.

"Do you have the stuff, Mr. Spenser?"

"So far," I said.

He smiled again and nodded. Everyone was silent. Westin looked at his watch. The two Fitchburg cops sat stolidly in their chairs. You don't have to be a cop long to get good at waiting.

Ronni Alexander said, "Are you married, Mr. Spenser?" Her smile when she asked me was very bright.

"No, ma'am."

"Ever?"

"No, ma'am."

She kept smiling and nodded as if she had confirmed a suspicion. If I'd been married, I'd have had better manners.

"Do you want me to demonstrate anything?" I said to Alexander. "Shoot the wings off a fly? Wrestle a bear? I'm really very skillful for an unmarried agnostic."

"Funny as hell too," Westin said.

"That's free," I said. "A fringe benefit, when you pay for the muscle."

"Well," Alexander said, "I'm afraid you'll do. I don't quite know why, but you're rather convincing. Think so, Ronni?"

Ronni did her brilliant smile. "I think inside he's really very, very nice. I'll feel much better with him aboard."

"Well, I guess you're hired then," Alexander said. "These gentlemen will brief you. Ronni and I will want to rest for an hour or so before we go to work again."

Alexander stood up. I stood up. We shook hands. Alexander and his wife went through the connecting door into their bedroom and closed the door behind them.

Abel Westin said to me, "You got some smart mouth, fella. You damned near blew the job."

"I know," I said. "My pulse is still pounding."

Farrell said, "Okay, okay. We gotta be in Lowell in two hours. You two talk with Spenser. Abe and I got things to do."

"I told you before, Farrell. My name is Abel, not Abe."

"Oh, yeah, right. Well, let's go see about getting a news conference organized."

Farrell shook hands with me. "These boys'll fill you in. Don't worry about Meade. He believes all that shit, but he's a stand-up guy, you unnerstand? He's straight ahead. And you better believe he's a winner. F. X. Farrell doesn't climb on the boat with a loser. Right?"

I nodded but Farrell didn't wait to see if I nodded or not. He jerked his head at Westin and they went out of the hotel room. I turned to the two cops.

They were both young. No more than thirty. One wore a houndstooth check jacket, the other a gray suit.

"You're Fraser," I said to the check jacket.

"Dale Fraser," he said. He was clean shaven and balding. He wore horn-rimmed glasses and looked like he might have played guard for a small college basketball team.

The other cop said, "Tom Cambell." He was blockier, with close-cut brown hair and a thick neck. His hands were small and very thick from palm to back. I shook hands with both.

"How do you feel about me coming in?" I said.

"Relief," Fraser said. "There was too much for two of us."

"How you been working it until now?"

"I been doing most of the coordination with local law enforcement. Tommy's been doing most of the bodyguard stuff."

"Most of the security provided by local cops, I assume?"

Fraser nodded. "I set it up ahead. Crowd control, screening people at receptions, that stuff. The personal safety, you know, carrying a piece and walking beside Mr. Alexander is our responsibility."

"We need more people?" I said.

Cambell said, "Not really. Now that you're on. We don't have to stand outside his door or anything. Dale calls ahead, arranges connecting rooms. He and I sleep next door. I mean ten more guys around him might help, but he won't stay inside a ring like that anyway. He shakes hands and"—Cambell shrugged—"he's trying to get elected, you know. You can't do that from hiding."

I nodded. "Okay, let's leave the set-up as it is. Dale, you keep doing the coordination. Tom and I will share the protection. You need anything, tell me. You have any suggestions, make them. I'm in charge but humble. No need to salute when you see me."

Fraser said, "Mind if we snicker every once in a while behind your back?"

"Hell, no," I said. "Everybody else does."

Chapter
3

In an auditorium at the University of Lowell, Meade Alexander was explaining where the nation had dropped its molasses jug and why. The room was mostly full. Ronni sat behind him on a folding chair on the stage, her knees and ankles neatly together. Her feet firmly on the floor, her white-gloved hands folded neatly in her lap, her eyes riveted on her husband, her interests animated and her expression approving, maybe even adoring.

"There is a crisis in this land," Alexander said. "Nearly half of the marriages in this nation end in divorce; what God has joined, any man can now put asunder at will."

I was leaning against the wall of the auditorium, near the stage, beside a window. When I looked out the window I could see the Merrimack River break over some rapids and drop in a waterfall before it moved off toward Newburyport. I had heard that someone caught a salmon in it not long ago. Or maybe that was another river, and I was being optimistic. At least it hadn't caught fire like the Cuyahoga River in Cleveland.

"My friends, nearly eighty percent of the video cassettes now sold are pornographic," Alexander said.

Some kid in the back of the room said audibly, "Right on."

Tom Cambell was on stage, in the wings, and Fraser was at the back of the auditorium standing beside the campus security chief, who had a walkie-talkie.

"Nudity and sex are big business. Any small grocery store in the land will sell magazines that twenty years ago would have landed the seller in jail. Television sells jiggle, newspaper columnists routinely suggest that any form of sexual excess is acceptable, that abortion is simply a matter of personal preference—as if the slaughter of unborn children were no more significant than an upset stomach."

The audience was a mix of students and faculty, with a few citizens of Lowell who were interested. Outside the auditorium there were pickets representing gay liberation, NOW, NAACP, the Anti-Nuclear Coalition, Planned Parenthood, and everyone else to the left of Alexander. Since, as far as I could tell, there was no one to the right of Alexander, it made for a considerable turnout. They were quiet by the standards I had learned in the late sixties and early seventies, but campus and Lowell city police had kept them at passive bay.

"The family, the nucleus of civilization, is under attack from the spread of feminism, from those who council a form of rebellion under the deceitful rubric of 'children's rights,' from drug pushers who would poison us, from those who would urge homosexuals to marry, from an intrusive government whose social workers all too often violate the sacred web of family with their theories of social engineering."

Beneath my window, on the grass, a young woman in a plaid skirt sat, leaning her back against a tree. A young man lay flat on the ground, his head in her lap. Each was reading, and as they read, her left hand absently stroked his hair.

"My candidacy is not merely political. I am striving not only to change laws, but to change the assumptions of a nation, to reinvigorate the purity and sinew of a younger America. To call forth the inherent decency in the people of this country, united under God, to refortify the resolve of this nation to stand firm against Godless communism. This is beyond legislation. I am calling upon all of you to join me in a crusade, to help me find America reborn."

There were four or five reporters down front who traveled with Alexander's campaign, heard him say America reborn, and opened their eyes, closed their notebooks, and stood up. They were halfway down the aisle before the applause sounded. Most of the audience stood to applaud and the applause seemed heartfelt. Here and there a professor shook his head, but the overwhelming body of the audience seemed to love what it had heard.

Alexander shook hands with the college president, who had introduced him. He faced the audience for a long minute with both hands above his head, then came down the stairs at the side of the stage. Tom Cambell came behind him and I closed to his side as we went up the aisle. Outside on the steps, there were some pictures taken of Alexander holding Ronnie's hand. Then into the cars and away from the campus.

Looking back out the rear window of the car, I saw the

young man and woman who had been reading on the lawn standing holding hands watching us go.

Twenty minutes later Alexander was sipping a cup of tea with milk and sugar and eating a pineapple pastry and telling several members of the Haverhill Republican Women's Club that the interference of the Internal Revenue Service with Christian schools was intolerable, as was our abandonment of Taiwan and our loss of the Panama Canal.

Ronni smiled, helped pour the tea, spoke briefly on the sacredness of the marriage bond and her conviction that her husband was all that stood between us and the arrival of the anti-Christ.

During this, Fraser circulated, keeping liaison with the local fuzz. Cambell and I tried to stay roughly on either side of Alexander. The only danger to him that I could spot were the pastries. I tried one and they tasted like something you'd swallow to avoid torture.

A smallish woman with short blond hair asked me if I was with Congressman Alexander. She wore a sensible gray suit and a corsage.

"Yes," I said.

"Well," she said, "we're all behind him up here. He's the first politician in this state to make sense since I've been voting."

"This is the only state that voted for George McGovern in 1972," I said. "You think a conservative can get elected in Massachusetts?"

"Absolutely. Massachusetts was just a little slower to come to its senses. But it has. Liberalism is bankrupt."

I was looking at her corsage. You don't see a corsage all that often, especially during the day. It was an orchid.

"Don't you love my corsage? Donald, my husband, gave

it to me last night when he knew I was going to meet the congressman. I kept it in the refrigerator all night."

I smiled. "It's certainly attractive," I said.

We left the Haverhill Republican Women's Club in time to get to the Raytheon plant in Andover for the shift change. Alexander stood at the gate and shook as many hands as he could as the workers came out heading for the parking lot. More than half the workers brushed by Meade and Ronni and ignored the outstretched hands. Some others shook hands without any sign of recognition. Most of the workers were men, and most of them turned after they'd passed Ronni and looked at her. A bearded worker in a plaid cap said, "Nice ass."

As soon as the four o'clock shift had stopped admiring his wife's backside, Alexander was back in the caravan and heading for a shopping mall in Peabody.

Alexander took up a position outside a Jordan Marsh store, across from Baskin-Robbins, and shook some more hands. Fix Farrell and Abel Westin kept herding people over toward him, and Alexander shook hands and smiled, and Ronni stood beside him and smiled.

A short woman with her gray hair tightly permed asked Alexander what he planned to do about the "darks."

Alexander said, "I beg your pardon?"

She said, "The darks. What are you going to do about them? They're getting in everywhere and we're paying for it."

Alexander said, "I feel the government has no business in education."

The woman nodded triumphantly. A young woman in over-the-ankle moccasins and gold-rimmed glasses said, "You're opposed to public education. You wish to abolish it?"

Abel Westin slipped between Alexander and the young woman. He said, "That's too complex a question for a forum like this, ma'am."

"But he said the government had no business in public education."

Alexander smiled. "We're preparing a position paper on that, my dear. When it appears I think you'll be satisfied."

"Good question though," Westin said.

The young woman said, "Bullshit," and went over to Baskin-Robbins for an ice cream.

From the shopping center we went to a reception at the Colonial Hilton Inn in Lynnfield. Alexander met with the Christian Action Coalition in a function room where jug wine, cheese spread, and Wheat Thins were served from a small buffet table along one wall.

Alexander sipped a small glass of wine, nibbled a Wheat Thin, and smiled graciously at the adoration that eddied about him like steam in a soup kitchen. All the men in the room wore suits and ties, all the women wore dresses and heels. There was a liberal sprinkling of gold jewelry among the women and a fair number of expensive wristwatches among the men. As the candidate spoke with the people, there were no questions, only shared certainties.

"You know what they're buying with food stamps? Cupcakes. I saw a woman in front of me at Star Market . . ."

"Do you know what they were reading in my kid's English class? Girls and boys both? You ever hear of Eldridge Cleaver?"

Ronni Alexander had a glass of wine.

"As long as the private sector has to compete with the government for money, the interest rates will stay up. It's simple supply and demand . . ."

I noticed that Ronni Alexander had finished her wine and gotten another.

The smoke thickened in the room. Born-again Christians didn't seem to sweat lung cancer.

". . . even have a Christmas pageant in school this year. Some Jew complained . . ."

Fix Farrell said to me, "Okay, we gotta get going. Ronni's started on the wine."

Ronni was getting her plastic cup refilled at the buffet.

Farrell muttered to Westin. "Make the fucking late announcement."

Westin said loudly above the room noise, "Excuse me, excuse me, folks."

Farrell moved over beside Alexander and whispered to him. Dale Fraser went out to get the cars brought up.

"Meade would stay here all night if we'd let him. But someone's got to be the bad guy. We have to get him to bed. So we thank you for coming, and if you'll just hold still a second, I know Meade will want to say good-bye. Then I hope you folks will stay and enjoy the wine."

Alexander stepped beside Westin and his smile freshened the thick air.

"I thank you all for coming. Remember me when it's time to vote. Listen to your conscience, and God bless."

Then he took his wife's arm. She smiled brilliantly, and with Farrell beside them and me and Cambell behind them, they headed out of the room and toward the waiting cars. Ronni had brought her plastic cup with her. One for the road.

Chapter
4

Back at the hotel in Boston, Fix wanted everyone to eat in their rooms, but Ronni wanted to try the new dining room, Apley's.

"Francis," she said. "I'm tired of being shut up in one room or another. I want some elegance."

Alexander nodded at Fix. "I'm sure it will be fine," he said. "Mr. Spenser can join us, if you're worried about security."

Farrell shrugged. "Your funeral," he said. "I don't eat that French crap myself."

The maître d' recognized Alexander and found us a table for three without trouble. Apley's was mirrored and elegant. A woman played a harp near the middle of the room. The menu was aggressively nouvelle cuisine.

The waiter took our drink order. I had beer. Alexander had a martini, and Ronni had a Jack Daniel's on the rocks.

Ronni looked at the menu and then smiled at me.

"Do you mind eating here, Mr. Spenser?"

"No. I like it. I eat French crap a lot."

The waiter brought the drinks. Alexander lifted his martini and smiled at us.

"Cheers," he said. We drank. "How do you like campaigning, Spenser?"

"On the whole, I'd rather be in Philadelphia."

"It can be tiresome, I suppose. Ronni and I have gotten used to it. And I must say there's a lift from . . ." He made a gesture with his hands as if he were packing a large snowball. "From being with the people. From actually seeing the voters."

"Including the young woman who asked about your stance on public education?"

Alexander smiled his splendid smile. "Politics is compromise, Mr. Spenser."

"You saw how she was dressed," Ronni said. The *s*'s slushed just a little.

"To try and articulate my position at that time, in that place, would not have been wise. She was obviously unsympathetic. The press was there. They'd like nothing better than to describe how I got into a shouting match in a shopping mall."

The waiter appeared. "Excuse me," he said. "May I tell you about our specials this evening."

Alexander nodded.

"First you can get me one more drink," Ronni said.

"Certainly, ma'am." The waiter took the glass, looked at Alexander and me. We shook our heads. The waiter departed.

"Tell us a bit more about yourself, Spenser. We know only that you come highly recommended, that you are unmarried, and agnostic."

"That says it all," I said.

"One of Francis's sources said you were, how did he put it, an ironist."

"That too," I said.

The waiter returned with Ronni's bourbon. She drank it while he explained about the specials. The explanation took a while and I wondered, as I always did when people recited a menu at me, what I was supposed to do while they did it. To just sit and nod wisely made me feel like a talk show host. To get up and go to the men's room seemed rude. Once in Chicago I had tried taking notes in the margin of the menu, but they got mad at me.

When the waiter got through, Ronni said, "Is that duck good?"

"Yes, ma'am."

"How about the stuff with the green peppercorns?"

"The game hen? Yes, ma'am, that's excellent."

"Which do you think would be better?" she said.

"Both are excellent, ma'am."

Alexander said, "I'll have the tenderloin of beef, please."

The waiter looked grateful. He looked at me. I ordered duck. He looked reluctantly back at Ronni. She finished her bourbon.

"I don't know what to have," she said.

The waiter smiled.

"If you'll bring me one more little glass of bourbon, then I'll decide." The last word sounded suspiciously like *de-shide*.

"Anything for you gentlemen?"

I had another beer. Alexander shook his head. The waiter departed. Ronni was studying the menu.

"I assume you have done police work at some time, Mr. Spenser?"

"Yes."

"You didn't like the police?"

"Yes and no," I said. "Like everything else. The work is worth doing, most of it. But"—I shrugged—"too many reports. Too many supervisors who never worked the street. Too much cynicism."

Alexander raised his eyebrows. "Too much cynicism? I would have thought you a cynic, Mr. Spenser."

I shrugged.

"You're not?"

"Not entirely," I said.

"What do you believe in?"

The waiter came back with Ronni's bourbon and my beer.

Alexander said to Ronni, "Why don't you have the game hen with peppercorns?"

Ronni swallowed some bourbon and nodded.

Alexander said to the waiter, "The lady will have the game hen with green peppercorns."

"Very good, sir. Would you care to order wine?"

Alexander said, "No, I don't think . . ."

Ronni said, "Oh, come on, Meade. Dinner without wine is like a kiss without a squeeze."

Alexander nodded at the waiter. He produced a wine list and handed it to Alexander. Alexander glanced through it and ordered a good California Pinot Noir. The waiter went to get it.

Ronni began to hum along with the harpist.

Alexander looked at me, finished his martini, put it down, and said, "So what is it you are not cynical about? What do you believe in?"

"Love," I said. "I believe in love—Alfie."

Alexander's face was serious as he looked at me. Ronni's humming was a little louder. The harpist was playing something classical that I didn't know. Obviously Ronni didn't know it either, but she wasn't discouraged. She swayed slightly with the music as she hummed.

Alexander kept his gaze fixed on me. "I do too," he said.

Chapter 5

Alexander was working a luncheon reception at the Marriott Hotel in Springfield. The crowd was stretch-fabricked and hair-sprayed and there were hors d'oeuvres and a cash bar. The hors d'oeuvres ran to bologna and cream cheese whirls, salami and cheese cubes on a stick, chicken livers and bacon. You could almost hear the arteries clogging as Alexander's supporters wolfed them down.

At one end of the room Meade and Ronni were in an informal reception line, shaking hands, smiling, cursing big government, and praising God. A young man and woman who looked like college kids stopped to talk with him. The boy had a mouse under his right eye. From where I was I couldn't hear them, but I saw Ronni's breath go in sharply, and I saw Alexander frown. He nodded then raised his eyes and looked around the room until he saw me. He gestured me toward him.

As I moved toward him through the crowd, a middle-aged man in plaid slacks said, "You can't just keep giving it away to people who won't work . . ." A woman in a bouffant hairdo and blue-rimmed eyeglasses said, ". . . Darwinism simply does not have the data to support . . ."

Ronni smiled at me brightly. Meade said, "Spenser, these two young people have a rather disturbing story to tell. I wonder if you could find a quiet corner and talk with them." He glanced at the two kids. "This is Mr. Spenser, our Chief of Security." I tried to look modest. "This is, ah . . ."

"John," the boy said. "John Taylor. This is my fiancée, Melanie Walsh."

I said, "How do you do," and took them to a sort of pantry off the reception room, where glassware and china and things were stored. I leaned against a stack of folded chairs and crossed my arms and said, "What's up?"

The kids looked at each other, then John said, "We're students. AIC. I'm a junior and Melanie's a sophomore. We were handing out literature yesterday for Mr. Alexander down by the Civic Center when a couple of men came along and told us to beat it."

I nodded.

"I said we were not doing anything illegal and what right had they to tell us to beat it. They just sort of laughed and then one of them knocked the bunch of flyers—Melanie had a bunch of Alexander flyers and we were handing them around, you know?"

I nodded.

"Anyway, one of them knocked the flyers out of Melanie's hand onto the ground and the wind blew them around and then I said something and the other one hit me and knocked me down."

"Johnny told them to leave me alone," Melanie said. "And they hit him before he was even ready and all his flyers blew around."

"And they said if she showed up there again, they'd do a lot worse."

"They tell you why they did that?" I said.

"No."

"Would you know them again?"

"Oh, yes. But they said if we told the police, they'd find us . . ."

I nodded. "Don't they always," I said.

John said, "I don't know, sir." Except for the mouse, he looked like a choirboy. Maybe a couple years older than Paul Giacomin.

"You folks born again?"

"Yes, sir. I accepted Jesus Christ four years ago. And Melanie found him this past year."

"How old were these guys?"

John looked at Melanie. Melanie said, "They were men, you know. Grown up. Thirty, forty years old."

John said, "They called Melanie a name."

"Don't they always," I said. Actually Melanie looked more like Dolly Parton than Aimee Semple McPherson, but the soul wears various vestments. "You have a right to pass stuff out down there without getting molested," I said. "If you're willing to try it again, I'll go with you and if the two gentlemen show up, I will reason with them."

"There're two of them," Melanie said.

"I know. It's not fair," I said. "But maybe they'll bring a couple of friends and even things up."

They both looked puzzled.

"Look," I said. "I'm really good at this kind of thing. I

can handle it fine. If you're willing, we'll get right to it. If they show up, I can surely persuade them of their sinfulness."

"I don't like them saying that about Melanie," John said. "But they were too big for me."

Melanie said, "I'll go."

I said, "Good," and went to check out with Cambell and Fraser. And Alexander.

"I'm not sure this falls under security, Spenser."

"Security includes intelligence, Mr. Alexander. I think this needs looking into. Tommy and Dale will cover it here. It's just up the street. I'll be back in an hour."

Cambell walked toward the door with me. "You sure you want to handle two of them by yourself?"

I nodded toward the ceiling. "Somebody up there likes me," I said.

"No need to make fun of us, Spenser," Cambell said. "It's serious for us."

"That's what you and Fraser are doing here," I said.

Cambell nodded. "Jesus is important in our lives. Because you don't understand it, no need to put it down."

I nodded. "I make fun of everything, Tommy," I said. "Even myself. No harm intended."

Cambell nodded again. "We could leave Dale here and I could drift down with you to the Civic Center," he said. "I hate to see a couple of kids get shoved around, myself."

"Me too," I said. "Next time it's your turn." We picked up some folders that had a picture of Meade and Ronni Alexander smiling on the cover. Then we left the Marriott and headed up Main Street.

Downtown Springfield was on the way back from hard times. The hotel was in a new complex called Bay State West that included stores and restaurants and walkways across Main Street to Steiger's and across Vernon Street to Forbes and Wallace. Up and down Main Street there were other buildings going up, but the marks of poverty and suburban shopping malls still scarred the older buildings. They stood, many empty, waiting for the wrecker's ball. The fate that they were born for.

On the corner of Court Street we stood with our backs toward the municipal complex and looked at the Civic Center. It seemed to be made of poured concrete curtains, with the square look that had been hot when it was built in the first flush of urban rescue. It fronted on Main Street. East Court Street ran alongside it to our left and a set of concrete steps went up to a landing from which an enclosed walkway stretched across East Court to the third level of a parking garage.

"We were handing stuff out there on the side, near the stairs," Melanie said.

"Okay," I said. "I'll go over in the garage. You start handing stuff out near the stairs and if these guys show up, you start retreating up the stairs and across to the garage. I'll be in the garage. Don't be worried. I can see you all the time."

They both nodded. John was having a little trouble swallowing. There was more pressure on him than there was on Melanie. He had a certain amount of manhood at stake. Or he thought he did.

"Don't do anything silly," I said to John. "I know you're mad, and I know you feel compromised that they pushed you and Melanie around. But you're not a big kid, and I am."

"Yesterday there were two of them and one of me," he said. "Today we're even."

His face was very serious. He had a short haircut, parted

on the left. He wore a red plaid shirt with a buttondown collar, chino pants, rust-colored deck shoes with crepe soles, and a tan parka with a forest-green lining. He probably weighed 155 pounds. He was probably an accounting major.

"Yeah," I said. "What are you majoring in?"

He looked surprised. "Finance," he said.

Close.

Melanie had on a black watch plaid jumper and a beige sweater, a full-length camel's hair coat, and black boots. She looked at John and said, "Don't be foolish, Johnny. I don't want you to get hurt."

"You can't just lie down and take it," he said.

"We won't," I said. "Let's get to it."

They went to the stairs. I strolled over to the garage. I'd have to be quick about things or John would get his clock cleaned proving he was manly. What happened to turning the other cheek?

You see one civic center you've seen them all, but the weather was splendid for November. Sunny, no wind, temperature in the low sixties—a grand day for scuffling. I had on a gray Harris tweed jacket and a black knit tie and charcoal gray slacks and a Smith & Wesson .38 Chief Special with a two-inch barrel, and cordovan loafers with discreet tassles. I was conservatively dressed, but when you take a size 48 jacket, the choices are limited. Especially if you insist that the fabric be animal or vegetable.

It was a twenty-minute wait before the two sluggers showed up. I knew who they were even before I saw the kids stiffen and glance toward me and then quickly away. Both were overweight, though neither was exactly fat, and I knew if the fight lasted more than five minutes, I had them. They were swaggering a little as they approached the kids, feeling pleased, thinking they would be having some fun. One of them wore a navy watch cap and a plaid flannel shirt with the sleeves rolled up to his elbows. There was a nude woman tattooed in blue ink on each forearm.

He said to the kids, "You didn't learn nothing yesterday, huh?"

His partner was a little taller and little less overweight. He had shoulder-length hair, streaked with gray.

Melanie started to move away from them, up the stairs, toward the walkway. John had to follow, keeping himself between the two sluggers and Melanie.

"Good idea," said the gray-haired slugger. "We'll talk in the garage."

The walkway was topped with a translucent amber plastic and they all looked a little yellowish as they walked across.

When they got across, there was no one on level three of the garage but me. The levels were color-coded. Mine was green. When the four of them walked into the little anteroom off the main garage floor, I was leaning against the far wall, by the elevators, with my arms folded.

"Hidey-ho," I said.

Tattoo said, "Who the fuck are you?"

I said, "I'm with the clean mouth bureau. Let's just step around the corner here and I'll explain why swearing is ignorant."

Tattoo frowned. He had come down here with Old Gray-hair to roust a couple of college kids and now he had something he wasn't comfortable with. Probably hadn't rousted a size 48 in a while. His partner took over.

"You a cop?"

I moved my head at the kids and we started into the garage while we talked. The two sluggers unconsciously stayed with us. I didn't look like a college kid, but there were two of them. And they were supposed to be tough. And it would be hard for them to explain to each other why one guy had scared them away. So they moved into the parking garage with us.

"A cop?" I said. "No, no. You misunderstand. I'm with the Alexander campaign."

We were fully into the garage now, and between two rows of cars. There was no one in sight.

The one with gray hair spoke again. "Alexander campaign, huh? Well, you probably know what we told these two nerds. Same goes for you."

"You a holy roller too?" Tattoo said.

"No," I said. "I'm a policy implementation specialist."

"What the fuck's that mean?" Gray-hair said.

I smiled very flutely. I said, "Well, it is campaign policy that our campaign workers not be harassed, if you see what I mean." I shifted my feet a little and got balanced.

"Oh, yeah." Tattoo again. "And what d'ya do if they are?"

I hit Tattoo a left hook. Maybe the best left hook ever thrown in Springfield. He went rattling back against a tan Buick Electra, and his knees buckled and he sagged without falling.

"Implementation," I said. And kicked the gray-haired man in the groin. He doubled up and fell down. Tattoo's eyes got a little clearer and he shoved himself off the Electra and lunged at me. Not smart. He lunged right into a straight left and stopped short. I shuffled a little to my right and came down over his left shoulder and hit him a right-hand shot that finished it. Tattoo dropped to the concrete floor and stayed.

John was just getting into his fighting stance as Tattoo went down. I smiled at him.

"There," I said. "The power of sweet reason."

Chapter 6

Alexander and I were sitting alone at a small table in the corner of the main dining room at a German restaurant called The Student Prince and The Fort. It was on Fort Street, which probably accounted for some of the name. Why it had all that other name was a mystery to me. But the food was good, and there was German beer, and I wasn't having a bad time.

Alexander ordered sauerbraten. I chose Wiener schnitzel. The restaurant was a splendid clutter of beer mugs and German artifacts. Susan and I had eaten there a couple of times before when she'd come to Springfield on business and I'd come for the ride. The food was good.

The waitress brought us two draft beers. Alexander looked down into the top of his as if there might be a message.

"You going to turn that into wine?" I said.

Alexander smiled without much pleasure. "That was

water, I believe. I know you don't mean any harm, but I'd rather not joke about Jesus, if you don't mind."

We are not amused.

I drank some beer. Alexander went back to studying his.

"You probably wonder why I wanted to have dinner with you alone," he said.

I nodded.

"Well, first, what did you learn about the two men that molested my young campaign workers?"

"I learned they had reached their limits with the kids," I said. "With me they were in over their heads."

"I heard you had a fight with them."

"Fight is too strong a word. I breathed heavily on them and they fell down."

"Even so," Alexander said. "I would have preferred another approach."

I shrugged. "Made me mad, slapping a couple of kids around."

Alexander nodded. "Did you learn why they did that?"

"They told me a man they didn't know gave them two hundred dollars to harass the kids. Said that he told them there might be more to come if they showed him they could handle it."

"A strange man just approached them on the street?"

I shook my head. "No, not quite. I called the Springfield cops, these guys have a modest reputation in what you might call paralegal circles. If you were from Boston or Worcester or Hartford and you wanted to hire a cheap small-time arm twister, the grapevine would lead you to these guys."

"Will the two young people press charges?"

"They said they would."

"What if these two men harm them, threaten them to make them withdraw the charge?"

"No," I said. "They won't. I told them not to."

Alexander looked up from his still unsipped beer. He studied me for a minute. "And they're afraid of you?"

"Um-hmm."

"Well, you are physically imposing, but there must be a savagery in you that doesn't show normally."

"Um-hmm."

Our waitress went by, and paused, and looked at my yearning eyes and empty glass.

"Would you like another beer, sir?" she said.

I nodded and she took my stein away and brought it back full very promptly. Alexander hadn't touched his yet. How could you respect a man like that?

Alexander looked at me some more. Probably checking for hidden savagery. "And there's no way to trace back who hired them?"

"I wouldn't say *no way*." I paused, sampled the second beer. It was in no way inferior to the first. "It could be investigated; the two sluggers could be pressed more vigorously. Maybe they'd remember more. Maybe not."

Alexander clasped his hands together and pressed his lips against the knuckles of his thumbs.

"What I am going to tell you, Spenser, is absolutely private. It is something that you must tell no one at all. No one."

I waited.

He looked back down at his beer some more.

"I have to confide in someone. I need help. I have to be able to trust you."

I waited some more. He looked up at me again. Piercing. "Can I trust you?"

"Sure," I said. "But the foreplay is getting tiresome."

He kept his piercing look on me. Must have spent hours getting it right. Probably a real purse-loosener at fund-raising speeches. Then he tightened the corners of his mouth, relaxed them, and said, "Yes. I will have to trust you. I must."

He waited for relief to sweep over me.

Then he said, "I'm being blackmailed. Now you see why I wondered who sent those thugs. I don't know who is doing the blackmail, but they wish me to drop out of the Senate race and throw support to my opponent."

"Browne," I said.

"Yes."

"You think he may be personally involved?"

"I don't know," Alexander said. "Obviously he's the one to benefit if I do as I'm asked."

I nodded.

"I don't know what to do," Alexander said.

I nodded again.

"Do you have any thoughts on the matter?" Alexander said.

"Not yet," I said.

We sat and looked at each other. Our waitress returned with dinner. We were silent while she set it before us, took my glass, went away, and brought it back full, and asked if we needed anything else.

Alexander said, "No thank you," in his Westbrook van Voorhees voice. The waitress departed. I took a bite of Wiener schnitzel. "Yum, yum," I said. I washed it down with a sip of beer. There were fried potatoes, and apple-sauce, and dark bread in a basket. I thought about the proper sequence for them. Maybe a rotating basis, a bite of schnitzel, a bite of potato, a taste of applesauce, some bread, a sip of beer. Then start over. Yes. That was the best approach, though one needn't be rigid. I had another bite of Wiener schnitzel. Drank some beer. Alexander was still looking at me. Didn't drink any beer, now he wasn't eating any sauerbraten. The man was mad.

"I will have to tell you, won't I."

"If I'm going to help you, you probably will," I said.

He looked down, took in a long breath, and closed his mouth and held it, and then let the breath out through his nose. He placed both hands, palms down, on the table and tapped his spread fingers once on the tabletop. Then he looked back up at me.

"It's Mrs. Alexander."

I nodded.

"She has, I'm afraid, been indiscreet."

I nodded some more.

"She has . . . they have . . ." His voice started to clog, and tears began to form in his eyes. He looked down again and breathed in several times, letting the breath out sharply, almost like a sprinter, trying to blow a little extra into his kick. Then he looked up again with his wet eyes and said quite steadily, "There are pictures."

"Oh, shit," I said. "I'm sorry."

He began to rock slightly in his chair, his hands still on the tabletop. "Videotape," he said. His voice was choked again. "Color." He stood up suddenly and walked away from the table toward the men's room. I sat and stared at the food. I didn't feel so much like eating anymore either.

The waitress came over and said, "Is anything wrong, sir?"

"Not with the meal," I said, "but my friend is ill. I think we'd better have the check."

"Yes, sir," she said. "I'm very sorry."

She was prompt with the check. I paid it. She went away and brought back the change. I tipped her.

"Thank you, sir," she said. "I hope that your friend feels better soon."

I shrugged. "The ways of the Lord," I said, "are often dark, but never pleasant."

She frowned slightly, and took her tip and went away.

Chapter 7

When Alexander came out of the men's room he looked very pale but his eyes were dry for the moment and he seemed back under control.

I said, "Let's take a walk."

He nodded. We walked up Fort Street. It was dark out and rainy now, but not very cold. I had on my leather trench coat and Alexander was wearing a poplin raincoat. The rain was light and not bothersome. Under other circumstances, in fact, it would have been good rain to walk in. Romantic. There were construction and demolition projects all around the lower Main Street area. Silent construction equipment gleamed in the rain, but not many people walked around. We turned up Main Street toward the Civic Center. Alexander had his hands in his pockets, his head bent, looking at the sidewalk as he walked. He wore a checked hat like Bear Bryant.

I said, "This is awful. I understand that. But I didn't

bring it up. If I'm going to help you with this, we have to talk about it."

Alexander said, "I know."

We passed Bay State West. There were a lot of people in the mall buying things. Recreational shopping.

I said, "I can fix this for you. Not all of it. Not what it feels like, but the other part. I can take care of the blackmail."

Alexander nodded. We passed Johnson's, its facade a dark green, the name in gold letters. A municipal bus stopped, let some people off, and moved on downtown.

"It was mailed to my home," Alexander said. "In Fitchburg. A videotape. VHS format. No return address, Boston postmark." We turned into Court Square, walking past the City Hall complex with its tower. There was a small park in the middle of the square. I was quiet. He had started. I knew he'd finish.

"I have a recorder, VHS. I played it one night while Ronni was out."

We turned left at the far end of the square. The closed end. Beyond was expressway. Beyond the expressway, the river, adding its damp smell to the rainy night.

"The film showed Ronni having sex with a young man in what appeared to be an apartment. It was apparent that she didn't know of the taping."

At the open end of Court Square, across Main Street, the Civic Center was glowing and bright. Its lights glistened off the wet buildings. The right kind of rain makes everything look good. Even the color-coded parking garage seemed attractive in the soft autumn rain.

"It was also apparent that it was Ronni. No possible mistake. I did not recognize the young man."

We turned right again, back onto Main Street, and kept

walking, away from the hotel. I wasn't wearing a hat. My hair was wet. Reflections of the traffic lights shimmered on the wet pavement. "Have you discussed this with her?" I said.

"No. She doesn't know. She's not to know. Ever. It would break her heart if she knew."

"I can't be delicate about this," I said. "The whole thing is indelicate. There's no way around it. I have to ask questions."

"Yes," he said. "Go ahead."

"You're persuaded that this is not a porno film, that is, something she posed for?"

"I'm sure that it is not deliberately posed."

"People don't just stroll around with videotape cameras," I said. "Someone set this up."

Alexander nodded.

"The room had to have enough light," I said.

"It was daylight mostly," Alexander said. "One wall of the room was glass and it was bright daylight. The drapes were open."

"Do you . . . has she . . . is there a way to narrow this down?" I said.

Alexander said, "I don't understand."

I took a deep breath. "Can we try to track down her partner or could it be any one of a number?"

Alexander stopped and squeezed his eyes shut and then turned his head away from me and down, almost the way a dog will cower. He tried to say something and couldn't. He tried again and still couldn't. His hands were deep in his raincoat pockets, his shoulders were hunched, and he rocked a little, as if a gentle wind were making him sway.

Finally he said, "I don't know," in a barely human voice.

"Can you ask her?" I said.

He shook his head.

The wind picked up a little and the rain, while it was still fine, was beginning to slant a bit as it came down, and drive in our faces. I turned my back to it. Alexander still stood swaying, facedown, unaware.

"If it came down to it," I said, "would you drop out of the race?"

Without looking up he nodded again.

"And never tell her why?" I said.

Nod.

"And throw your support to Browne?"

Nod.

"I've heard Browne is mob-connected."

Nod.

"And you'd support him?"

Alexander's shoulders were beginning to shake. He raised his face. Tears were squeezing out of his squinted eyes and running down his face.

"Yes," he said. His voice shook, but there was an energy in it I had never heard before. He straightened a little and stopped swaying. The rain came harder and the wind intensified. It was no longer a good rain to walk in. Even under other circumstances. It had gotten cold, as if November had reasserted itself. We were alone on the street, with the wind driving the rain before it.

Blow, winds, and crack your cheeks!

"I would support Satan to spare her," Alexander said. I nodded. "So would I," I said.

Chapter 8

It was nearly midnight when we got back to the Marriott and went up with the water dripping off us and making small puddles on the elevator floor. Outside the door to his suite Alexander paused and looked at me. His eyes were a little red, but other than that he had it back together.

"We'll be returning to Washington through the holidays. I don't use Christmas to campaign," Alexander said.

I nodded.

"I want her free of this," he said. "Remember that priority. It is the only absolute you have. She is to be free of this."

I nodded.

"And she's not to know."

I nodded.

Alexander put out his hand. I took it. We shook hands. Alexander stood a minute holding on to my hand after we'd finished shaking. He started to speak, stopped, started again, and then shook his head and released my hand. I nodded.

"I have to trust you," he said. "I've no other hope."

Then he went into the suite and I went next door to the room shared by Cambell and Fraser. I knocked on the door. When Fraser opened it I said, "Alexander's back. I'm going to bed."

Fraser nodded, closed the door, and I went to my room on the other side of Alexander's.

In the morning Alexander told Cambell and Fraser that I was doing a special assignment for him and that they'd have the full security responsibility henceforth. I rented a car and drove ninety miles back to Boston and straight to Morrisey Boulevard. It was twenty of eleven when I pulled into the visitors' parking space in front of the *Globe*. It was ten of eleven when I was sitting in the straight chair beside Wayne Cosgrove's desk in the newsroom.

"This a social call," Cosgrove said, "or are you undercover for the *Columbia Journalism Review*?"

"No, I came in to lodge a complaint about the *Globe*'s white-collar liberal stance and they directed me to you."

Cosgrove nodded. "Yes," he said. "I handle those complaints."

"Well, what have you to say?"

"Fuck you."

"Gee," I said, "words must be your business."

He grinned. "Now that we're through playing, you gonna tell me what you want?"

"I want everything you have on Robert Browne."

Cosgrove was tall and narrow with curly hair and glasses and a blond beard. He wore a three-piece suit of dark brown tweed, and a dark green shirt and a black knit tie. The vest gapped maybe three inches at his waistline and his green shirt hung loosely out over his belt buckle.

"The congressman?"

"Yes."

"Why?"

"None of your business."

"Christ, how can I resist?" Cosgrove said. "You're so charming when you need something."

"Can you dig it out for me? You're computerized. How long could it take?"

"Yeah, sure, I can get it up for you, but being as how I'm in the news business, I can't help wondering if there might not be something, you know, newsy, about a guy like you wanting everything we have on a U.S. congressman."

"And senatorial aspirant," I said.

"Senatorial aspirant? Jesus Christ. Want a job on the editorial page?"

"I need to know anything I can about Browne," I said. "I won't tell you why. Probably never will tell you why, and I'd rather no one knew I was interested."

"Well, that sure sounds like a good deal for me," Cosgrove said. "Meet me someplace tonight, around six thirty, and I'll give you what I got."

"Ritz bar," I said. "I'll pay."

"You should," he said. The phone rang and Cosgrove picked it up. I got up waved him good-bye and went out.

I turned in the rental car and walked to my office. It was still raining, steady and cold now. No longer pleasant. The office was stale from emptiness and I opened both windows while I went through my mail. Across the way the art director was in residence and I blew her a kiss from the window. She smiled and waved. The mail was not worth opening. I dropped it all in the wastebasket. Maybe I should get an unlisted address. What if I did and nobody cared? I called the answering service. There were no messages. I sat down in my swivel chair and took out my bottle of Irish whiskey and had a drink. The cold wet air from the window behind me blew on my neck. I thought about lunch. I looked at my watch. Twelve twenty-five. I had another pull on the bottle. I looked at Susan's picture on my desk. Even filtered through a camera I could feel her energy. Wherever she was things coalesced around her. I made a small toasting gesture with the bottle.

"Like a jar in Tennessee," I said out loud.

I drank another shot of whiskey and looked at my watch again. Twelve thirty already. I put the cap back on the bottle and put it away. Lunch.

I walked up to a Mexican place on Newbury Street called Acapulco and had a plate of enchiladas and three bottles of Carta Blanca. Then I walked to my apartment on Marlborough Street and went in and aired it out. There was a letter there from Paul Giacomin. Things were good at college. He was going to spend Thanksgiving with me, and he might bring a girl friend.

Whiskey, enchiladas, and beer did not make for a lively afternoon. At 1:15 I lay down on the bed to read *Legends of the Fall*. About 1:30 I rested my eyes for a moment and at 3:20 I woke up with the book still open on my chest and the thick taste of empty calories in my mouth. I got up and took a shower and put on sweat pants and a waterproof jacket and ran along the Charles for an hour until my blood moved once again without protest through my veins and the guilt of sleeping during the day was dissipated. Then I went over to the Harbor Health Club and worked on their new Nautilus until I felt sure of redemption and it was time to see Wayne Cosgrove.

I arrived at the Ritz bar freshly showered, shaved, and pleasingly exhausted at 6:20. I had primped for the Ritz bar, which was one of the few places in the city where ties are required and jeans are barred. I had on my brand new corduroy jacket with leather buttons and a tattersall shirt and a dark blue knit tie that picked up the blue in the tattersall. I took off my leather coat as I walked into the Ritz lobby and checked myself in the mirrors near the bar. With my gray slacks and my cordovan loafers I was fit for permanent display. My gun was tucked away on my right hip out of sight. I thought about getting a tweed holster but decided it would jeopardize my credibility.

The bar was uncrowded and I got a small table near the window where people passing on Arlington Street could look in and assume I was closing an important deal. Cosgrove hadn't arrived yet. When the waiter came I asked for a Rolling Rock Extra Pale in the long neck bottle. They had none. I had to settle for Budweiser. Even the Ritz bar must disappoint occasionally.

I had finished the first bowl of peanuts and managed to choke down three Budweisers when Cosgrove showed up. He was wearing the same outfit he'd had on earlier except he'd added a long plaid woolen scarf. He carried a big thick manila envelope.

"Sorry I'm late," he said. "Knowing it was the Ritz I had to go home first and brush my teeth."

"I don't mind," I said. "It just meant more peanuts for me."

Cosgrove sat down and handed me the big envelope. The waiter appeared. Cosgrove said, "Martini, stirred not shaken, twist of lemon."

"No olive?" I said.

"Only a fucking beast would have an olive in his martini," Cosgrove said. "Olives are packed in brine, ruins the taste."

"I figured the gin and vermouth had already done that."

Cosgrove shrugged. "No accounting for taste," he said.

"You prove that," I said. "What's the scarf for?"

"Strangling muggers," Cosgrove said. "You still working for Meade Alexander?"

"You've been busy," I said.

"Are you?"

"Yes."

"That why you want the Browne stuff?"

"No comment."

The waiter brought Cosgrove's drink and a fresh bowl of peanuts. He looked at me. I shook my head. I'd only been redeemed for a half an hour.

When the waiter left, Cosgrove took a sip of his martini, looked pleased, put the glass down, and said, "No fucking comment? You work a week for a politician and you're walking around saying no fucking comment?"

"You're right," I said. "It's embarrassing. Ask me again."

"You investigating Browne for Alexander?"

"I don't want to answer that question," I said, "and if you ask it again, I'll beat your teeth in."

Cosgrove nodded. "Better," he said. He drank some more martini. "How's Susan?" he said.

"She's away," I said.

Cosgrove started to speak, looked at me, stopped, and then said, "I wouldn't have thought Meade Alexander was your style."

"I don't think he is," I said.

"On the other hand," Cosgrove said, "who is your style,

except maybe that goddamned African assassin you hang around with."

"Hawk," I said. "I'll tell him you said that."

"That was on deep background," Cosgrove said. "How come you're working for Meade Alexander?"

"Best offer I had."

"How's Mrs. Alexander?"

"Fine."

"Hear she drinks a little."

"Don't we all," I said. "Know anything worth telling about the Alexanders?"

"We having dinner afterward?"

"Sure."

"I'll think on it," he said, and sipped more martini.

Chapter 9

We ate in the café.

"Ronni Alexander drinks. We both know that," Cosgrove said. "She drinks too much and when she does she gets boisterous, and sometimes mean. When I was in the Washington bureau it was sort of a common joke."

"I picked up some of that," I said. "Why haven't I ever read about it?"

Cosgrove ate some scrod. "We do news, not gossip. Or we try to. The fact that a congressman's wife's a boozer isn't news unless it involves her in something that is news, you know?"

"And I gather it didn't."

"Not that I ever knew. They live in Georgetown. She didn't spend much time in public with him. When she did usually she'd be on good behavior. And the staff was very alert."

"No other scandal?"

Cosgrove shook his head. "Nope."

"What kind of congressman is Alexander?"

Cosgrove sipped a little white wine. "Disaster," he said. "He really is a born-again fundamentalist Christian. And that limits him. His options are so proscribed by his convictions that he can't legislate very well. He's not a big thinker either. He's impatient with complicated issues because he doesn't understand them. Often he doesn't even know they're complicated."

"What's his chance of getting elected to the Senate?"

"Possible."

"In Massachusetts? I thought this was the most liberal state in the country."

"The national media says that because we went for McGovern in '72. It's bullshit. Some parts are liberal, some parts are conservative. But the statewide mood these days, as us political analysts say, is conservative, bedrock, down home,   let's-get-back-to-the-old-verities-and-truths-of-the-heart—that shit. Bobby Browne's a traditional liberal—social programs, government money, federal mandates. Keynesian economics. Straight New Deal Democrat." Cosgrove shrugged. "Most people are saying fuck that. Guy paying twenty percent interest wants a change. Browne's a continuation. Hell, Eddie Moore hand-picked him when he decided to retire."

I was having broiled scallops with lemon butter. I ate some.

"So you think Browne has reason to worry."

"Yes."

"Who's the paper backing?"

"Browne. Jesus Christ, Spenser. Meade Alexander once wanted to ban the teaching of evolution in the public schools."

I nodded.

"I mean, U.S. senators are supposed to be worrying about how not to have a nuclear war. Alexander worries about unisex bathrooms and jiggle television."

"He honest?" I said.

"Who, Browne or Alexander?"

"Either."

"Alexander's honest. He's so honest he makes your teeth hurt. I don't know about Browne. Most of them aren't. Honesty in a public servant is overrated."

"How about Farrell?"

Cosgrove grinned. "Old Fix. Fix thinks he's John Wayne, carries a fucking gun, for crissake. But he's hot these days. The world is coming closer to Fix's point of view. If Fix has one. He's been the resident fascist on the City Council for twenty-two years and he believes in counting heads and calling in favors and paying off debts. He believes in getting even. He believes in arm-twisting and buttonholing and rabble-rousing. When Alexander surfaced in the Senate race, Fix jumped aboard early. All that piety gives Fix a good tone, and if Alexander makes it, things will pick up for Fix. One thing I'll give him, he knows how politics work."

"He refers to your employers as the Boston Glob."

Cosgrove grinned again. It pleased him. "Yeah, I know. You gotta love old Fix. He's almost perfect."

Cosgrove finished his wine. The waiter removed our dishes, offered us dessert. We declined.

"Brandy," I said.

"Sure. How about in the bar. Makes me feel upscale."

I paid for dinner and we went back to the bar. It was fuller than it had been. Tables were occupied, so we sat at the bar. Cosgrove had Galliano. I had brandy and soda.

"Good thing about Fix is he knows he's a lout. Stays

out of the way when Alexander's talking to the Dover-Sherburne Republican Club, you know. Lets Westin handle the press. Fix knows that if the Friends of the Wenham Library spent ten minutes with him, they'd call the cops."

Cosgrove drank his Galliano, and put the glass down and looked at his watch.

"Gotta run," he said. "Mary gets home from class at nine."

I nodded.

Cosgrove said, "Anything you want to tell me about Browne, or Alexander, or anybody, you just give me a call, buddy. You know where I am."

I nodded again. "I'll be in touch," I said.

Cosgrove left and I sat at the bar and had another brandy and soda. But I never liked sitting alone at a bar, so after I finished the second one I paid the check and went home.

Chapter
10

The rain had stopped. The streets were dry. I sat in my office with the morning sun coming through the window and read through the clips and Xerox copies and computer printouts that Wayne Cosgrove had assembled for me. My office was quiet.

I didn't know what I was looking for. I hoped I'd know it when I saw it. There were interviews with Browne, the text of speeches, editorials endorsing him, columns speculating on his future, columns assessing his performance, news stories covering his participation in key house votes and floor maneuvering, pictures of Browne at ribbon cuttings and tree plantings.

I felt like I was studying for an exam in a subject I didn't like. The office felt hot. I opened the window a crack and the November draft was cold on my back. I closed the window. Read in sequential mass like that, the news coverage of Browne's career became an immersion course in politics. As I read I realized that no one took it seriously, in the sense that one takes, say, love, seriously. Everyone took it seriously the way they take baseball seriously. The question was of performance, of errors made, of runs scored, of wins and losses. Rarely was the question of substance discussed. Was Browne good or bad? Were the things he did good for people or bad for people? These questions disappeared behind a tone of journalistic objectivity. The excitement was: Would he win the election or lose it? Was his support of legislation calculated to help his chances or hurt them? Was the vote in Congress a defeat for the President; was it a victory for the House leadership? Even the editorials tended to judge politics in terms of a contest, or victory and defeat.

At noon I went out and got a roast beef sandwich with chutney on whole wheat bread and a cup of black coffee and brought it back to my office. I ate in the silence and drank my coffee and looked occasionally at Susan's picture on my desk. *Let us be true to one another, dear.* I read some more reportage. I looked at pictures of Browne at ship christenings and fund-raising parties. I even read the text of a couple of his speeches. Somebody, maybe Adlai Stevenson, had said that wanting to be elected disqualifies you for the job. I read some excerpts from the *Congressional Record.* I read a letter to the editor that Browne had written to the *Worcester Telegram.* I looked at a picture of Browne shaking hands with an eagle scout. I studied the ADA rating list where Browne received good marks.

At 2:30 I went out and bought another cup of black coffee and brought it back to my office. I read some more. What kind of a man wanted to be in politics? Was it possible to be a good man and do politics? Maybe not. I drank some of the coffee. Swiveled my chair and stared out the window. Maybe it wasn't possible to be a good man and do anything. The afternoon sun reflected off the windows across the way and I couldn't see in. I didn't know if the art director was there today. Maybe she could see me. I waved, in case. Maybe being a good man didn't amount to anything anyway. It didn't seem to get you much. You ended up in the same place as the bad men. Sometimes with a cheaper coffin.

I looked at Susan's picture again. I drank the rest of my coffee and dropped the empty cup into the wastebasket.

"The sea of faith is at its ebb, babe," I said out loud to her picture. Her picture smiled its elegant, devilish smile and made no comment.

At about 4:15 I saw it, and when I did I knew it. It was a picture of Robert Browne among a group of men and women. The caption said it was after he'd spoken at a 1978 fund-raising dinner in Rockland. Browne was smiling and shaking hands with a portly white-haired man in a double-breasted suit. Browne's wife was beside him, smiling as hard as he was. There were well-dressed men and women crowded in the background and in among them a face that I recognized. Vinnie Morris.

Vinnie Morris worked for Joe Broz. What made that interesting was that Broz was the sole owner and proprietor of a large and successful mob. Vinnie was what you might call the executive assistant.

I wanted to say, "Oh, ho." But it would have sounded odd in the empty office. Maybe I ought to hire an assistant, so when I said, "Oh, ho," someone would hear me. A dog might suffice. I could look knowingly at the dog and say, "Oh, ho," and the dog would wag its tail, and I'd give it a cookie.

Vinnie was Broz's instrument. He had no life of his own. If he was at Browne's fund-raiser, it was because Broz sent him. If Broz sent him, it was because there was business to be done. Broz would have the same interest in politics as Exxon does in oil wells.

I wrote Joe Broz on a piece of note paper and read some more. I read until 9:15 and there was nothing else. I stuffed all the clippings and Xerox copies and photos back into the big envelope and put the envelope into the bottom drawer of my file cabinet. Then I sat back down at my desk and looked at my notes. *Joe Broz.* Not a lot of notes for twelve hours research.

I put the note in my pocket, stood up, and looked out the window at the dark street and the empty buildings. I was hungry. I got out my bottle of Irish whiskey and had a drink. I was still hungry. I capped the bottle, put it away, and went home. I had a steak, a bottle of red wine, and went to bed. The wine helped me to go to sleep but not to stay there. I woke up at 3:30 and lay awake and thought disjointedly about life and death until dawn.

Chapter 11

The morning was clean and cold and bright. I bought a corn muffin and a large black coffee at the Dunkin' Donut shop on Boylston Street and stood out front, on the corner of Exeter Street, and had breakfast. It was early. People with clean shaves and fresh perfume were going by on the way to work. They all walked with hurried purpose, as if they were all late for work. I dropped my empty cup into the trash and strolled down Boylston. I turned up Berkeley past my office building toward Police Headquarters. It was just after eight when I went into Martin Quirk's little cubicle off the homicide squad room.

Quirk looked like he'd been there for hours. His sleeves were rolled up, his tie loose. There was a half-empty container of coffee on the desk. When I came in Quirk nodded.

I said, "Good morning, Martin."

Even with his tie loose and his sleeves rolled, Quirk looked, as he always did, brand new. As if he'd just come from the Mint. His coarse black hair was short and freshly cut. His face was clean shaven. His shirt was gleaming white and crisp with starch. His gray slacks were creased. The blue blazer that hung on a hanger from a hook on the back of his door was unwrinkled.

He said, "You want any coffee?"

I said yes and he went into the squad room and brought me a cup and a refill for himself.

"How's Susan?" he said when he was back behind his desk.

"She's away," I said.

He nodded.

I said, "I'd like to take a look at your intelligence file on Joe Broz."

"That's the Organized Crime Unit," Quirk said. He drank more coffee. His hands were very thick and the fingers were long and blunt-ended.

"I know," I said. "But I don't have any friends over there."

"And you think you have friends over here?" Quirk said.

"Everything's relative," I said. "At least you know who I am."

"Whoopee," Quirk said. "Why do you want to see it?"

"I think he owns a politician."

Quirk grinned. "Everyone else does," he said. "Why shouldn't Joe?"

"I want some evidence."

"Don't we all. Explain things to me. If it sounds good, I'll get you the file and you can sit here and read it."

I leaned back a little, put one foot up on the edge of Quirk's desk, and told him. He listened without interrupting, his hands locked behind his head, his face blank.

When I finished he said, "I can get the names of the two stiffs you rousted in Springfield."

"And?"

"And?" Quirk frowned. "Christ, are you getting senile? And maybe they'll lead you somewhere. Maybe they got sent around to remind Alexander that whoever was blackmailing him was serious. A message."

I nodded.

"Yeah," I said. " 'Don't think I'm kidding, see what I can do if I wish.' That kind of message."

Quirk smiled. "See, if you apply yourself, you can do it."

"Okay, get the names. Might be worth talking with them again. How about the file? Give me something to do while you're talking to Springfield."

I spent three hours looking at the file that OCU kept on Joe Broz. I was looking for intersections between Browne and Broz. I found none. The only intersection I found was between Alexander and Broz. Broz's eldest son went to Georgetown University. When Congress was in session, Alexander lived in Georgetown. It didn't look like a clue.

When I left, Quirk said, "How come you haven't told me to keep all this to myself?"

"I didn't think I needed to," I said.

Quirk handed me a piece of paper with two names and addresses written on it. "The two stiffs in Springfield," he said. "I told the Springfield cops you were cooperating with me, unofficially, on an investigation."

"Well, it's sort of true," I said.

"Sure it is," Quirk said. "While I was out of the office you didn't steal my jacket. If that's not cooperation, what is?"

"Thanks for the use of the file," I said.

"Let me know how things go down," Quirk said.

"Sure," I said.

When I got back out on the street it was nearly time for lunch. After I ate it, there'd be only five or six hours to kill before supper. No wonder I hadn't thought about the Springfield stiffs, busy as I was. Even now there were decisions to make before I could drive out to Springfield. Should I eat before I left? Or stop at a HoJo on the Mass Pike?

I stopped in Cambridge and bought a brisket, pastrami, and Swiss cheese sandwich on a roll at Elsie's to eat on the way. The art of compromise—maybe I was political after all.

Chapter 12

The two Springfield sluggers were named Pat Ricci and Sal Pelletier. I decided to go alphabetically. Pelletier lived in a brick apartment building on Sumner Avenue near Forest Park. He didn't answer my ring, so I went back out and sat in the car and debated whether to call on Ricci or wait for Sal. While I was debating, Sal showed up, walking briskly along the sidewalk with a paper sack of groceries in his arms. He was the one with the tattoos.

I got out of the car and walked toward him. He didn't recognize me. I said, "Remember me?"

His eyes widened. He said, "Hey."

I said, "We need to talk. Shall we go to your place?"

"What do you want to talk about?" Sal said. He moved away from me as he talked.

"I was hoping you'd show me your tattoos," I said.

"Take a walk," Sal said. "I got nothing to talk about with you."

I could see the top of a quart bottle of Miller High Life

beer sticking out of the grocery bag. I took it out and dropped it on the sidewalk. It broke and the beer foamed around the broken glass.

"Hey, what the fuck are you doing?" Sal said.

"It could be you and not the bottle," I said. "I want to talk."

Sal dropped the bag and turned and ran. I jogged along after him. He didn't look in shape and I figured he wouldn't last long. He didn't. He turned into the park and 100 yards past the entrance he stopped, gasping. I jogged up and stopped beside him.

"Oughta take up running gradually," I said. "Starting all out like that is dangerous."

Sal was sweating in the cold November sunshine, and his face was red.

"Whyn't you leave me alone," he said. "I didn't hurt them kids."

"Sal," I said, "let us cease to play grab-ass. I want to know some things from you, and you are going to tell me."

Sal's chest was still heaving.

"Remember how hard I can hit," I said.

Sal nodded.

"Who hired you to roust those two kids?" I said.

Sal opened his mouth, and closed it, and shook his head. I shrugged and hit Sal a modified version of the left hook I'd hit him with before. It sat him down.

"I can hit you with that left hook until evening," I said. "Who hired you to roust those kids?"

Sal's head sank forward. "Nolan," he said. "Louis Nolan."

"Who's he?"

"A guy around."

"He connected?"

Sal nodded.

"Who with?"

Sal shook his head. "I don't know," he said. "He's just connected, you know? He's one of those guys that's in touch with the big boys. You know that. Everybody knows that. He asks you to do something, you're glad to do it. Glad to do him a favor, you know?"

"So he told you to lean on these kids?"

"Not them kids especially. Just any Alexander person. Didn't matter who. Whoever was handy."

"Why did he want that done?" I said.

"Said he wanted to send Alexander a message."

"What message?"

Sal shood his head again. "He don't tell guys like me anything he don't have to. Just give us the deuce and said to get it done."

"Where do I find Louis Nolan?"

"You won't tell him you got it from me?"

"You don't tell him I'm coming," I said, "I won't tell him I saw you."

"Wheeler Avenue," Sal said. "Up Sumner past the X." He gestured the direction. "I don't know the number."

I said, "Thanks, Sal, see you around."

He was still sitting on the ground when I turned down Sumner Avenue toward my car.

I drove up Sumner Avenue. When I passed the X-shaped intersection Sal had mentioned I started looking for Wheeler Avenue. I almost missed it. It wasn't much of an avenue. It had been overnamed. It was a short residential street that ran one block between Sumner and Allen Streets. I drove past it a little ways and stopped at a drugstore and looked up Louis Nolan in the phone book. The number was 48. I drove back and turned up Wheeler Avenue.

Forty-eight Wheeler Avenue was a modest white Cape with a one-car garage, at the Allen Street end of the block. I parked on Allen Street in sight of the house and looked at it. Nothing happened. I looked some more. Same result. No clue appeared.

I got out of the car and walked to the house and rang the front doorbell. Inside I could hear a vacuum cleaner. I rang the bell again. The door opened and a man in a suit and vest said, "Yes?"

His white hair was in a crew cut and his white mustache was trimmed close. He was middle-sized and blue-eyed and erect.

I said, "Mr. Nolan?"

He nodded. His face was pink and healthy-looking and his eyes were bright and opaque, like polished metal.

"Vinnie Morris sent me," I said.

He nodded again and gestured with his head into the house. I went in. He closed the door behind me. The living room was to my left, the dining room to my right. A plump woman about Nolan's age was vacuuming the living room. Nolan gestured me toward the dining room.

"Kitchen," he said. "Want some coffee?"

"No, thanks."

We walked through the dining room and into the kitchen. The house looked like it had been built in the thirties. The kitchen counters were still surfaced in black rubber tile. The yellow porcelain gas stove was on long, curved legs.

We sat at the kitchen table. The vacuum continued to hum in the living room. Nolan took a black leather cigar case from his inside coat pocket and offered me a cigar. I shook my head. He took one out and bit off the end, spitting the fragment into the sink without leaving the chair.

"Fruit or anything?" he said.

I shook my head again. Everything in the kitchen shone as if it were on display. Nolan lit his cigar with a fancy lighter, put the lighter into the pocket of his vest, let some cigar smoke out, and said, "Okay."

I said, "Vinnie's a little"—I shrugged and wobbled my hand—"about the two stiffs you hired to rough up Alexander's people."

"Which two stiffs?" Nolan said.

"Come off it, Louis," I snapped. "Pelletier and Ricci. You think you're talking in court?"

"What went wrong?"

"Well, you know, how smart is it to slap around a couple of clean, cute college kids, for crissake. It gets people mad. Was that what Vinnie wanted done?"

Nolan shook his head.

"What'd Vinnie want done?" I said. "He want to make people mad?"

Nolan shook his head again.

"Did he?" I said.

"No."

"What did he want done?"

"Shake 'em up a little," Nolan said. "Let 'em know we mean business."

"And what happens?" I shook my head disgustedly. "The two stiffs get their ass handed to them. The cops come. You gotta bail them out. How does that make us look?"

Nolan said, "I didn't know they'd have some pro from Boston with them."

I leaned forward a little and said it again. "How does that make us look?"

"Bad," Nolan said.

"You goddamned better believe it," I said. "And it don't make Vinnie happy, and you know who else it don't make happy?"

Nolan nodded.

"Who don't it make happy?" I said.

"Mr. Broz."

I stood up. "Keep it in mind," I said. Then I turned and walked back out through the dining room and opened the front door and walked to my car and drove away.

I'd found out what I wanted to know, and, as a bonus, I'd made Nolan sweat. Spenser, master of deceit.

Chapter 13

When I got back to my apartment it was quarter to eight in the evening and Paul Giacomin was there. He was lying on the couch reading a *New Yorker* and drinking a long neck bottle of Rolling Rock Extra Pale.

"You're right," he said when I came in, "this stuff is habit-forming."

"World's best beer," I said. "How are you?"

"Good," he said. "You?"

"Fine," I said. "You eat yet?"

"No."

"I'll make something."

He came out into the kitchen and sat at the counter while I looked into what was available. Rolling Rock Extra Pale was available, and I opened one. Paul had grown since I had acquired him. He was maybe a shade taller than I was now, flexible and centered.

"You're looking in good shape," I said. "You working hard?"

"Yes. I dance about four hours a day at school, and a couple of times a week I go into New York and work at a gym called Pilate's."

"The money coming?"

"Yes, my father sends it every month. Just the money, no letter, nothing. Just a check folded inside a blank piece of paper."

"Ever hear from your mother?"

He nodded. "I get a letter every once in a while. Pink stationery, tells me that now I'm in college I have to be very careful in choosing my friends. Important, she says, not to get in with the wrong crowd."

"How about pasta?" I said. "Supplies are low here."

I put the water on to boil and sliced up some red and some green peppers and a lot of mushrooms. Paul got another beer and opened one for me too.

"You happy with Sarah Lawrence?" I said.

"Oh, yeah. The dance faculty is very professional. A half hour from New York, you can get people."

I stir-fried the peppers and mushrooms with a little olive oil and a dash of raspberry vinegar, cooked some spinach fettuccine, and tossed in the peppers, mushrooms, and a handful of walnut meats.

Paul and I ate it at the counter with grated Jack cheese and half a loaf of whole wheat bread that was left in the cupboard.

"How about the wrong crowd," I said. "You getting in with them?"

"Not much luck," Paul said. "I'm trying like hell, but the wrong crowd doesn't seem to want me."

"Don't quit," I said. "You want something, you go after it. I was nearly thirty-five before I could get in with the wrong crowd."

We opened two more Rolling Rocks. The last two.

"My fault," I said. "It's what happens when you let your work interfere. How long you home for?"

"Over Thanksgiving," he said. "I go back Sunday."

"Thanksgiving is tomorrow," I said.

"Yes."

"There's nothing to eat."

"I noticed," Paul said. "Maybe we can go down to the rescue mission."

I finished the last Rolling Rock. There was a bottle of Murphy's Irish Whiskey in the cupboard above the refrigerator for emergencies. I got it out and had some on the rocks. "I'm glad to see you," I said.

"Hard booze?" Paul said.

I nodded. "Want a sniff?" I said.

"Sure."

I poured a little for him, over ice. He sipped it and didn't look completely pleased.

"Is it worse than drinking nothing?" I said.

"No."

I put the dishes into the dishwasher and wiped off the counter. We went into the living room with two glasses and the whiskey and some ice.

"Since when have you been drinking hard booze?" Paul said.

"It's come to seem soothing lately."

Paul nodded. "One of those all-hour convenience stores will probably be open," Paul said. "I could run out and get some sliced turkey roll and a loaf of Wonder bread. Maybe a quart of Tab, for the festive board."

"We'll eat out," I said. "The hotels are usually open. The Ritz, maybe." I drank some whiskey. When you've been nursing it out of a bottle neck, a glass and ice seems like being on the wagon. "I thought you were bringing a girl friend."

"Paige, yeah. I was. But her parents got bent out of shape, so she went home."

There was a fire laid in the cold fireplace. It saved time in case I met someone who wanted to jump on my bones in front of a romantic fire. I'd gotten this one ready in August. No sense wasting it. I got up and lit it and sat back down and watched the flames enlarge. The hell with romance.

I drank some more whiskey. Paul nursed his. I knew he didn't like it. My glass was empty. I added more whiskey. An ice cube.

"Susan still in Washington?" Paul said.

"Yes."

"Couldn't get back for Thanksgiving?"

"Nope."

"I'm surprised you didn't go down."

I nodded.

"Where is it she's at?"

"Children's Hospital National Medical Center," I said. "One Eleven Michigan Avenue, North West, Washington, D.C., 20010."

"Internship?"

"Yes. Pre-doctoral internship." I leaned forward and poured a little whiskey into Paul's glass. The kindling was fully flamed and the larger hardwood logs were beginning to burn. I stared at the flames as they flickered over the wood. Matter is neither created nor destroyed. $E = mc^2$.

"She quit being a guidance teacher?"

I nodded. "Actually took a leave, but she's not likely to go back. Not with a Harvard Ph.D. in psychology."

"You mind?" Paul said.

"Her quitting guidance?"

"The whole thing," Paul said. "Ph.D., internship, off to Washington, not around for Thanksgiving. You mind that?"

I got up and walked to the window and looked down into Marlborough Street. It was bone empty. "Susan is doing something very important to her," I said. "She needs to do this, to strive, to seek, and not to yield."

The holiday desolation of the empty street was depressing. In the streetlights' shine it was manifestly silent. Over the hills and through the woods to grandmother's house we go.

Paul said, "Yeah, but do you mind?"

I drank some more whiskey. "Yes," I said.

"How come you didn't go down for Thanksgiving dinner with her? She have to work?"

"No. She's spending it in Bethesda with the head of her intern program. It's important to her." I kept staring out the window.

"More important than being with you?"

"There's other times," I said.

A cab came up the empty street and stopped on the other side. An old woman in a fur coat got out carrying a fat white cat. The cabbie pulled away and she walked up the dark steps to her door and fumbled at the lock and then went in.

"If you had something you were working on, you'd stay away on Thanksgiving," Paul said.

"I know."

"If I'd gotten a chance to dance, like at Lincoln Center or something, I'd have gone. I wouldn't have come here."

"Sure," I said. My glass was empty. I went and got the bottle and poured some more. I filled it before I remembered the ice. Too late. I sipped some neatly. Paul was watching me. A grown face, not a kid. Older maybe than eighteen because of the psychological experience he'd had and overcome.

"You went off to Europe without her in 1976."

"Yes." My voice was hoarse. More whiskey, relax the larynx. Good thing I hadn't used ice. Throat needed to be warmed.

"It's killing you, isn't it?"

"I want her with me," I said, "and more than that, I want her to want to be with me."

Paul got up and walked over and stood beside me at the window and looked out. "Empty," he said.

I nodded.

He said, "We both know where I was when you found me, and we know what you did. It gives me rights that other people don't have."

I nodded.

"I'm going to hurt you too," he said. "We're the only ones that can, me and Susan. And inevitably I'll do it too."

"Can't be helped," I said.

"No." Paul said. "It can't. What's happened to you is that you've left Susan inside, and you've let me inside. Before us you were invulnerable. You were compassionate but safe, you understand? You could set those standards for your own behavior and if other people didn't meet those standards it was their loss, but your integrity was . . ."—he thought for a minute—". . . intact. You weren't disappointed. You didn't expect much from other people and were content with the rightness of yourself."

I leaned my forehead against the cold window glass. I was drunk.

"And now?" I said.

"And now," Paul said, "you've fucked it up. You love Susan and you love me."

I nodded with my forehead still against the window. "And the rightness of myself is no longer enough."

"Yes," Paul said. He took a large swallow of whiskey. "You were complete, and now you're not. It makes you doubt yourself. It makes you wonder if you were ever right. You've operated on instinct and the conviction that your instincts would be right. But if you were wrong, maybe your instincts were wrong. It's not just missing Susan that's busting your chops."

" 'Margaret, are you grieving,' " I said, " 'over Goldengrove unleaving?' "

"Who's that?" Paul said.

"Hopkins," I said. "Gerard Manley Hopkins."

"There's a better one from *The Great Gatsby*," Paul said. "The part just before he's shot, about losing the old warm world . . ."

" 'Paid a high price for living too long with a single dream,' " I said.

"That's the one," Paul said.

Chapter 14

It was the Monday after Thanksgiving, Paul was back at Sarah Lawrence College. I was back in my one-room office with a view of the art director on the corner of Berkeley and Boylston. It was 9:15 A.M. and I was reading the *Globe* and drinking some coffee. Today was the day I would have only two cups. I drank the last of the first one when my office door opened and Vinnie Morris came in. Behind him came a large blank-faced guy with a hairline that started just above his eyebrows.

Vinnie was my age, a good-looking guy with a thick black mustache and his hair cut sort of longish over the ears. He was wearing a black continental-cut suit and a white shirt with a white tie. His camel's hair coat was unbelted and hung open and the fringed ends of a white silk scarf showed against the dark suit. He had on black gloves. The big guy behind him wore a plaid overcoat, and a navy watch cap on the back of his head like a yarmulke. His nose was thick, and there was a lot of scar tissue around his eyes.

"Vinnie," I said.

Vinnie nodded, took off his gloves, put them together, and placed them on the top of my desk. He sat in my office chair. His large companion stayed by the door.

"You got any coffee?" Vinnie said to me.

"Nope, just finished a cup I brought with me."

Vinnie nodded. "Ed, go get us two coffees," Vinnie said. "Both black."

"Hey, Vinnie," Ed said. "I ain't no errand boy."

Vinnie turned his head and looked at him. Ed's septum had been deviated enough so he had trouble breathing through it. I could hear the faint whistle it made.

"Two black," Ed said.

"Large," I said.

"Two large," Vinnie said.

Ed nodded and went out.

"Slipping punches wasn't his long suit," I said. "You still with Broz?"

Vinnie nodded.

"Joe send you over?" I said.

Vinnie shook his head.

I leaned back in my chair and waited.

"You been in Springfield?" Vinnie said.

I nodded.

"You been making a pain in the balls of yourself in Springfield?"

"It's the least I can do," I said. "Spread it around."

Vinnie nodded patiently. "Want to tell me what you been doing out there?"

"No."

"It's one of the reasons I like you, Spenser. I can always count on you to be a hard-on. Really consistent, you know. A hard-on every time."

"Well, if I ever fail you, Vinnie, it won't be for lack of trying."

Vinnie grinned. There wasn't a lot of warmth in the grin, but it seemed real enough. It was probably as warm as Vinnie could get.

Ed came back in with the coffee in a paper sack. He'd bought one for himself. I wondered if that was considered exceeding orders. Rebellious bastard.

"Thanks, Ed," I said when he put mine on the desk. I took the cover off and put it into the wastebasket, then I reached over and took Vinnie's cover and dropped it into the wastebasket. I sipped some. First sip of the day's last cup. Coffee got me sort of jumpy lately. Time to cut back. Man of iron will, no problem. I'd begin cutting back today.

Ed tore a little half circle out of the cover of his coffee. He put the torn-out piece back into the empty bag and put the bag on the corner of my desk. I took it and put it into the trash. Neat work space, orderly mind. I drank the second sip of my last cup of the day. Ed slurped some of his coffee through the hole he'd torn in the cover.

Vinnie said, "You went and talked with Louis Nolan. You told him that I sent you. How come?"

"I wanted to see if he was connected to you and Joe."

"And?"

I shrugged. "And he is. He jumped up and lapped my face when I mentioned your name. Offered me some fruit." I sipped more coffee and smiled at him. "And here you are."

"You know more than that," Vinnie said. "You know he put those two stumblebums to work on my job."

"Yes," I said. "I do know that."

"So, what do you make of it?"

"You wanted Alexander's attention," I said. "You wanted to remind him of the kind of folks he was dealing with. So you had Louis hire a couple of local biceps to lean on anyone at all in Alexander's campaign. Couple of college kids were easy, and the two stiffs went for them."

Vinnie looked at me for a long minute. Without moving his eyes he said, "Ed, wait in the corridor."

Ed turned and went out and closed the door behind him. Vinnie got up and moved his chair around so he was sitting beside me.

"What do you figure we want from Alexander?" he said. His voice was soft. Ed couldn't hear it if his ear were flat to the door.

"I figure you want him to lose."

"Because?"

"Because you have a piece of Robert Browne and you and Joe like only sure things."

Vinnie nodded thoughtfully. I drank a bit more coffee. Two cups a day was plenty.

"You're still good," Vinnie said. "You always been good, and you haven't slipped any."

"Kind of you to say, Vinnie."

"How'd you make the connection?"

"Saw you in the background of a Browne campaign picture."

"What made you look?" Vinnie said.

"Somebody interferes with Alexander's campaign," I said. "Browne's a logical suspect. I just started looking at everything I could find on him."

Vinnie drank some coffee. I wondered if he needed to cut back. He was about my age. Looked healthy, but you never could tell. You wake up one day and find you have to cut back on coffee. Scoundrel time.

Vinnie was shaking his head. "You wouldn't go to the trouble," he said. "You wouldn't trace it all the way back to me just over a couple of gofers getting jostled."

I waited. Vinnie was thinking things over. There was a little coffee left. I drank half of it. If I always drank just half of the remainder, it would never run out.

"Okay," Vinnie said, "we're in it. You know we're in it, and I'm betting you know how far."

I smiled.

"You know we got the films of Mrs. Alexander."

I smiled again.

"Alexander told you, and sicked you onto it. You came back from Springfield and did your research because you figured it was Browne okay, but not because of the small scuffle we organized. Because of the films. He show you the films?"

I smiled.

"Get a look if you can. Broad's really something—got an excellent-looking bush. Anyway, you did your research, saw that picture, went out to Springfield, and did what you did."

I drank the last of the coffee. Half each time was only a theory. Like a tree falling soundlessly in the woods.

"It was a mistake," Vinnie said. "Hassling Alexander's staff was a mistake. But . . ."—he spread his hands—"spilt milk. The question we have before us, you might say, is where do we go from here?"

"If you drink too much coffee, doesn't it bother you?" I said.

"No, drink it all day. Doesn't do a thing. You want Ed to get some more?"

"No."

"So where do we go, Spenser?"

"Maybe I can try tea, or some of that decaffeinated stuff."

"Stop," Vinnie said. "That stuff's slop. Coffee or nothing is the way I go."

I nodded.

Vinnie said, "Besides your problems with caffeine, you got any thoughts on our situation?"

"You got something on Mrs. Alexander and I want it and you don't want me to have it," I said.

"And we don't want you trying to get it," Vinnie said.

"But I'm going to get it anyway."

Vinnie nodded. "We could go public with the films if you get annoying."

"And then you've shot your hold on Alexander," I said. " 'Freedom's just another word for nothing left to lose.' "

"Yeah, but his chances of election are zilch."

"Maybe not," I said. "Maybe he rises above it. Maybe it backfires and people suspect Browne of the whole thing and give Alexander the sympathy vote."

It was warm in my office. Vinnie got up and took off his overcoat and folded it carefully over the back of my other office chair.

"And maybe it brings in the cops and the feds," I said, "and everybody's investigating the blackmail and they look more closely into Browne and you've lost your tame congressman."

Vinnie pursed his lips and shrugged.

"And you've thought of all that," I said, "or you'd have done it already. You wouldn't be here."

"And if Alexander were willing to go that route, he wouldn't have you gumshoeing around looking into it," Vinnie said.

"Maybe," I said. "Or maybe he won't unless he has to.

I say we have a standoff. You blow the whistle on Mrs. Alexander, and I'll blow the whistle on Robert Browne."

"'Course we could kill you," Vinnie said.

"Hard to do," I said.

"But not impossible," Vinnie said.

"Can't prove it by me," I said. "But say you do, what happens then?"

"People look into it," Vinnie said. He was looking out the window as he spoke, and a small thought-wrinkle appeared vertically between his eyebrows. "I don't know how many people you've talked with about Browne's connection. Knowing you, not many. Still, we buzz you and people will wonder. That goddamned nigger could be bothersome."

"Especially when I mention that you called him a goddamned nigger."

Vinnie shook his head and made a slight pushing gesture with his hand. "It's the way I talk," he said. "I know Hawk. Something happens to you, he'll be a royal pain in the ass till he gets it straightened out."

I waited. Vinnie thought some more. Then he smiled.

"So for the moment, say we don't buzz you. We still got things our way. We got Browne in our pocket, and if he loses, then we got Alexander in our pocket, 'cause we got the films."

"So far," I said.

"So far," Vinnie said. "We'd rather have Browne, all things being equal. He's in place, and we know him, and he's not as stupid as Alexander. But Meade would do in a pinch."

"He'll be pleased with the endorsement," I said.

Vinnie grinned his cold, genuine grin. "He'll have to be," he said.

I thought about things after Vinnie left. It didn't sit right, none of it.

I'd thought up a lot of good reasons why they didn't just go public with Ronni in the buff, but they didn't persuade me. The reasoning was too subtle for Joe Broz. Broz was old-fashioned and direct. His idea of finesse was to wire a bomb to your ignition. He wouldn't pussyfoot around with this. He'd spread the picture around and expect Alexander to go down the tube. And he'd be right. Alexander's constituency would not swallow having their hero married to the Whore of Babylon. And his opponents would be so heartened and amused that Alexander couldn't get elected to Cuckolds Unlimited. I knew something Vinnie didn't. I knew that Alexander would go in the tank for them rather than let his wife be smeared. I looked at my watch: ten of eleven. Too early for Irish whiskey.

The more I thought about things, the more they didn't make any sense. It wasn't Broz's style. It wasn't even Vinnie's. It was about Ed's style. It was something that should have been simple and was being complicated. Usually when that happened to something I was trying to figure out, it meant that there was too much I didn't know.

Why didn't they just use that film? Why the fancy blackmail? It didn't make sense. Not Broz's kind of sense. It made amateurish sense. But Broz was not amateurish. I looked at my watch again. Eleven o'clock. I had to see the film. I didn't like to ask, but I had to. I had nowhere else to go. I spent some time reassuring myself that my interest in the film was simply professional. And it was. Completely. Like a doctor. Detached. Maybe if I got an early flight to D.C. I could watch the movies in the afternoon.

I called Alexander's office in Washington and told him that I was coming down and why. Then I pulled out my typewriter and wrote up what little I knew about things. It took one page, double-spaced. I folded it up, put it into an envelope, sealed the envelope, and took it over to the Harbor Health Club to leave with Henry Cimoli.

Henry had a problem with T-shirts. If he got them big enough for his upper body, they tended to hang down to his knees like a dress. If he got them the right length, he couldn't get his arms through the sleeves. He'd solved it so far by getting the right length and cutting the sleeves off, but as his health club got tonier and tonier, he'd begun to look into custom tailoring.

"If anything happens to me, give it to Hawk," I said. "Otherwise don't open it."

"Can't be a list of the people who don't like you," Henry said. "Envelope's not thick enough."

"It's my secret formula," I said. "How to be more than five foot four."

"I'm five six," Henry said.

"So how come when you fought Sandy Sadler he kept punching you on the top of the head?"

"I was trying to bull inside," Henry said.

I went home to pack.

Chapter 15

Alexander's Washington home was a three-story yellow frame house on the corner of Thirty-first and O Streets in Georgetown. He let me in.

"Ronni's away for the afternoon," he said. "It's in the den."

He led the way. The house was elegant Victorian, entirely immaculate. The den was fireplaced, paneled, leather-chaired, and hokey. There was a bison head mounted on the wall above the fireplace.

Alexander said, "You know how to operate one of these?"

I said I did. The videotape player was in a cabinet under the television. The connection wires ran up behind the cabinet.

"The tape is in there," Alexander said. "Everything is on. Simply push the play button."

He handed me a key. "Lock the room while you are

watching. When you are through leave the tape in the recorder and lock the door. I have another key."

I nodded.

"I'm going to work," he said.

I nodded. He paused at the door to the den, looking at me. He started to speak and stopped. His face looked hot.

I said, "I'm sorry I have to do this."

He looked at me another moment then went out and closed the door behind him. I went and locked it and left the key in the lock, then I went back and pushed the play button and sat in a leather chair and looked at the TV screen.

There was an interval of blank screen then some miniature polka dots against a black background and then a full-face medium shot of Ronni Alexander. She was doing a kind of inexpert dance, her arms above her head, her hips swaying. The sound cut in, not very clearly, as if the microphone were too far away, but I could hear that Ronni was humming as she danced, and, by listening hard, I could tell that she was humming "Night Train." I felt itchy with embarrassment. She danced past a table and picked up a glass, the shallow kind that people serve champagne in and shouldn't. She drank off the contents and threw the glass against the wall. Still dancing, she unbuttoned her blouse and slowly peeled it off. She was looking at someone in the room. I couldn't see much of him. Just the back of a dark head with a very expensive haircut. Ronnie unbuttoned her skirt at the side and slid the zipper down and held it momentarily with a look of contrived coquettishness, then let it drop. She wasn't wearing pantyhose. She was wearing underpants and stockings and a garter belt. A garter belt. Jesus Christ. The last garter belt I could remember was the year Mickey Mantle won the Triple

Crown. She took off her bra. She unsnapped her garters and rolled her stockings off, one at a time, slowly, still making pseudodance movements and humming "Night Train." She drank several more glasses of champagne and tossed the glasses away. Tempestuous. Finally she slid out of her last garment and was naked. I thought of Alexander watching this and my throat felt tight.

"You bitch," I heard myself say aloud in the quiet, ornate room. My voice sounded more sad than angry. Her partner became part of the scene now, a soft-faced young man with a mustache, maybe a few years older than Paul Giacomin. He stretched out on the bed and let her undress him. I could hear scraps of their dialogue. What I could hear made me wish for "Night Train." I was glad the mike had been badly placed.

When they were both naked they had sex. They did more than that. They put on a clinic. Ronni's dance had been artless, but her sex was expert. She did things I had rarely contemplated, though nothing I objected to. And she made a good deal of noise while she did it. Her partner clearly enjoyed himself, but he was also careful to arrange her full face to the camera as often as possible. He wore sunglasses during the entire performance.

When the tape ended it simply ended, there was no dramatic resolution, it merely stopped *in medias res*. I rewound the tape and played it again. This time around I noticed that the room was brilliantly lit by sunlight and at one brief shot saw an uncurtained window wall off camera right. Most of the action seemed to take place on a double bed with a pale blue comforter on it. The champagne was on a bureau. In the background on a bedside table was a clock radio, with a digital display. The time seemed to be 2:08. With the sun shining in like it was early afternoon it meant the windows faced west or southwest depending on the time of year. From their clothing I couldn't tell the time of year.

The camera must have been concealed behind the mirror over the bureau. It covered the whole room from there, though its focus was on the human activity. In another shot there was a desk, apparently on the window side of the bed. I ran the tape back and forward over the desk several times. There were books on the desk, but the spines were turned away and I couldn't make out a title. There were pens and pencils in a beer mug. There was also a Smith-Corona portable electric typewriter. I rewound and ran the tape again. There was an emblem and lettering on the beer mug. I couldn't make it out. I found a magnifying glass in the drawer of a rolltop desk and tried again to read the mug as it drifted by on the screen. But I couldn't. The glass merely reduced the picture to its component dots. The best I could do was see that it looked like one of those mugs they sell in college bookstores with the college or fraternity emblem on them.

I ran the tape three more times, but there was nothing else to get from it. Ronnie seemed drunk. She postured in some childish fantasy of Salome; she was skillful in all of her sexual activity, but a little self-conscious about it, and her companion patronized a very good barber and wore sunglasses while screwing. The action looked to be in someone's bedroom, not a motel, and the bedroom had a western exposure, probably not at ground level or they would not have left the shades open, even for camera light. Unless Ronni was even more unusual than I thought.

I rewound the tape one more time, left it in the machine, shut everything off, closed and locked the door to the den, and let myself out Alexander's front door.

I knew why he'd left me there alone. I was glad he had. My rental car was parked on O Street. I got in and drove a short block to Wisconsin, turned left, and headed in-town. I hadn't learned much, and I'd embarrassed my client and myself. I was getting used to that.

Chapter 16

I had taken a room at the Hay Adams. When I was alone I was a Holiday Inn man. But I was hoping for some time with Susan while I was here, and Susan was worth the Hay Adams. My room overlooked Lafayette Park and beyond it the White House. I hung up my clothes and had room service deliver a couple of beers and *The Washington Post*. Then I called Susan at her hospital. I could feel tension buzz in my stomach while I dialed. Of course she was with a patient, and of course she couldn't be disturbed. I left word that I was at the Hay Adams if Ms. Silverman got a moment free from succoring the afflicted.

Then I stood for a while and drank my beer and looked out at the White House. A guard leaned against one of the columns on the front porch. The people with the signs had them propped up against the fence out front. On the lawn to the right a television crew was filming a stand-up with the White House in the background. The President was in there somewhere, and the First Lady. She was there too, with the President. She wasn't off someplace far studying to be a doctor.

I got tired of looking at the White House and sat down in one of the chairs and put my feet on the double bed and read the *Post*. By the time I finished the *Post* it was getting dark outside. I looked at the White House some more. I could go for a walk, but if I did, I might miss Susan if she called.

I turned on the TV and watched the early news and wondered why the early-news people in every city were wimps. Probably specified in the recruitment ads. *Early-News Person Wanted. Must Be Wimp. Send resume and tapes to* . . . I shut off the television and looked out the window some more. I could order up some Irish whiskey and get drunk. But if Susan did call . . . It was dark now and the White House gleamed in its spotlights. I thought about Ronni Alexander trying to be Yvonne De Carlo and the look on Alexander's face when he left me there to watch. I thought about the lucky people that Susan was treating. Her undivided attention for fifty minutes. Son of a bitch.

They were having a party at the White House. Limousines pulled up the circular drive and let people out. Some people didn't come in limousines. They simply walked up the driveway. Maybe they took a cab. I'd always wondered how you said that. *Sixteen Hundred Pennsylvania Avenue, my good man, and don't spare the horses*. The President and the First Lady were probably dressing. Or maybe they were necking. Or . . . Someone knocked at the door of my room. I went and opened it and there was Susan wearing a silver raccoon coat and carrying a bottle of champagne and smelling like Eden in springtime.

"Did you really say 'succor the afflicted' to the department secretary?" she said.

"Yeah," I said. "I think she was offended."

I stepped aside and she came in and put the champagne on the bureau and turned and smiled. I stood and stared at her. There were times when I wanted to strangle her. But never when she was with me. Her presence overcame everything.

"Jesus Christ," I said.

She opened her arms and I stepped in against her and hugged her. She raised her face and I kissed her. I felt liquid and dispersive, as if I might dissolve into the floor.

Susan was brisk and cheerful. "Now you have a decision to make," she said. "Do you want to drink the champagne before or after you jump on my bones?"

That was easy.

Afterward we sat up in bed drinking the champagne from water glasses.

"See," Susan said. "I do succor the afflicted."

"Yes," I said. "You give good succor."

Susan drank some of the champagne.

"Was Paul with you on Thanksgiving?"

"Yes. We ate out. How about you?"

"Super. There were five or six of us from the program and John, our supervisor, had us all out to his home in Bethesda. There were twenty-five people in all, including some very big people in the profession."

"Yeah, but how many of them can do a one-armed push-up?"

Susan smiled and drank more of her champagne. "Tell me about what you're doing down here," she said.

"Besides seeking succor?"

She nodded.

"I'm working for a congressman," I said.

"You? That doesn't seem like you."

"Maybe it was an excuse to get to Washington," I said.

"I wouldn't think you'd need an excuse."

I shrugged. "Anyway," I said, "I'm working for a congressman named Meade Alexander."

"Meade Alexander? Good God, what does he think of you?"

I poured the rest of the champagne evenly into our two glasses. "He has not been fortunate in his marriage," I said.

Susan settled back a little against her pillows and I told her about Meade and Ronni Alexander.

When I got through, Susan said, "The poor woman."

"I hadn't thought too much about that," I said. "I've been kind of identifying with Alexander, I suppose."

Susan nodded. "She must be very desperate."

"Most people are," I said.

Chapter 17

I dropped Susan off at 8:15 the next morning in front of the Medical Center on Michigan Avenue.

"When you come to work wearing the same clothes, won't people suspect you of shacking up?" I said.

"I hope so," Susan said.

"Want me to pick you up after work?" I said.

She shook her head. "I can't until late," she said. "There's a staff cocktail party. They have one every month on the assumption that morale will be uplifted."

I nodded.

"I'll make a reservation for nine," I said. "Any suggestions? It's your city, not mine."

She shook her head. "No, I'd trust you with a restaurant reservation in Sri Lanka."

"Everybody's good at something," I said. "I'll pick you up here."

"Yes." She kissed me good-bye carefully, so that her lipstick didn't smear, and then she was out and off to work leaving the smell of her perfume to gloss up the rented car.

I drove back intown on North Capitol Street and then took M Street out to Georgetown.

Georgetown is nearly gorgeous. The buildings are elegant, the setting along the Potomac is graceful. You can run along the tow path of the old Chesapeake and Ohio canal and you can eat and shop and drink along M Street and Wisconsin Avenue with the heartening certainty that you're chic. Like L.A. and New York, the dining and drinking spots were ornamented with the possibility that you might see somebody famous. Even if it was a politician.

I parked the car in the lot of a Safeway on Wisconsin Avenue. Early winter in D.C. was around fifty and pleasant. I went across the street and bought a cup of coffee to go in a small food store that advertised empanadas in the window, but didn't have them made yet for the day. I strolled along Wisconsin Avenue and thought about a plan. The more I thought about it, the more I didn't have one. I could work on my restaurant selection for tomorrow evening. But that didn't do much for Meade and Ronni. Maybe there wasn't much to be done for Meade and Ronni. I stopped at the corner of Reservoir Avenue to sip on my coffee. Only the second cup of the day. Then I went on. I couldn't talk with Ronni. I couldn't even let on that she wasn't perfect. I had gotten all I was going to get from Vinnie, and Vinnie was the town crier compared to Joe Broz. The last communication I'd had from Joe Broz was some years back when he told me he was going to have me shot. Not many people follow up on a promise anymore. I knew that Broz had a copy of the videotape of Ronni's indiscretion. I didn't know how he'd gotten it. I finished my coffee and looked for a place to throw the cup.

Littering in Georgetown was probably a capital crime. Maybe if I reconstructed it. Broz had purchased Robert Browne some years back. This year Browne's position seemed threatened by Meade Alexander. By a means not yet apparent, Broz had some tapes of Mrs. Alexander and he sent a copy to Meade and told him to drop out. He had probably, though not certainly, been responsible for the death threats that had got me hired in the first place. And he was demonstrably responsible for the two hoods in Springfield who had roughed up the kids. I could look into Broz's candidate, Browne, but even if I nailed him, Broz would still have Alexander as long as he had the indiscreet tapes. And my business was to save Ronni's reputation. The rest was unimportant. I understood that. I even agreed with it. I reached the corner of M Street and turned right. If I got the tape back, it didn't solve much. There was no way to know how many copies there were, or even if Ronnie had made others. There was no guarantee she wouldn't make another one. Across M Street there was something called the Market. I crossed and went in. It was a miniature version of the Quincy Market building in Boston, a collection of small food stands quaintly housed in an old brick building. I bought some coffee from a young woman wearing a red checked kerchief for a headband and a white T-shirt that said HOYAS above the college crest. The T-shirt was tight and the lettering in HOYAS was somewhat distorted. I read it carefully. A detective learns to study things. It was still early and the place was nearly empty. I cruised through, looking at all the food and wrestling with the urge to sample everything. Iron control won again and I went out with only my black coffee. One more cup wouldn't hurt. I could stop in on my way back, after I'd walked some more and thought of a plan: A victory lunch. I'd have one of everything and maybe make small talk with the young woman and her T-shirt. HOYAS. A pugnacious bulldog wearing a derby had been on the flat lands of her abdomen and thus unbent. I turned down a side street and walked to the canal. Two joggers moved along the tow path at an easy pace. I'd seen the crest before on a beer mug in the tape of Ronni Alexander. I stopped dead. My coffee was half drunk. I stood stock still and finished it in small sips. Georgetown University. Joe Broz. Ronni Alexander. A plan?

I went into an ornate high-rise shopping mall where everything was marble and gilt and looked like something left over from Caligula's birthday. Hidden down by the washrooms were a couple of utilitarian phones and under them hung some D.C. phone books. I looked under *B* and there he was—Gerald Broz with a Georgetown address. How many Brozes could there be? I found the number for the dean of students' office at Georgetown University and called and asked if they had a Gerry Broz in the college. They said they did. I asked if they could give me his address and they said they couldn't, but if I would leave my name and number they'd ask Mr. Broz to call me. I said never mind and hung up. My plan was taking shape. It was a little soon to go back to the Market and eat everything, but I'd keep it as a goal. A man's no better than his dreams.

I checked Gerry Broz's address in the phone book, then went back out and strolled west on M Street. Gerry's place was on the corner of M and 35th Streets opposite Key Bridge. It rose three stories on the north side of M Street and looked out at the Potomac through window walls at each level. Perfect for indoor videotaping by daylight. Even the first floor insured privacy, for it began above a three-car garage on the street level. I went over and looked at the mailboxes. It was three apartments, one per floor, and G. Broz occupied the top. I went back out and stood on the corner. The D.C. weather wasn't pleasant anymore. It was cloudy and the temperature had dropped and the wind had picked up. Compared to Boston in December it was like a morris dance, but for D.C. it was chilly. I turned up the collar on my leather trench coat. I looked at the apartment some more. It began to rain, and the temperature being what it was, it mixed some snow in. I moved a little closer to the wall of the liquor store on the corner where I was standing. Did Boston Blackie spend a lot of time standing on the corner in a freezing rain saying to himself, *Now what?* He did not. As time went along I seemed to be doing more of it. *The rightness of myself isn't enough anymore. How would an eighteen-year-old kid know that? Thoughtful little bastard. Probably didn't waste a lot of time standing on cold corners thinking,* Now what?

I could burgle the apartment, but what would that get me? I wouldn't know till I burgled it. If he caught me, he'd know I was onto the tape business, although if he was involved in it, and it was a hell of a coincidence if he wasn't, he knew that already. Vinnie would have spoken to Broz and Broz would have spoken to Gerry. I decided it was better than what I had been doing, so I went across the street and rang Gerry Broz's bell. No one answered. I rang a long time to be sure. Gerry was probably in class. Probably discussing Savonarola and the Italian Renaissance, or pointing out the errors of Malthusian economics.

The outside door was easy. It took less than a minute. But Broz's apartment door was not easy. It was clearly a special lock, specially installed, and it was better at staying locked than I was at picking it. The door was special too, and I knew I wasn't going to kick it loose. I went down one flight and knocked at the door of the second-floor apartment. No answer. The door had a conventional lock.

When I was inside with the door closed I went directly to the window wall, opened the sliding doors, and went out on the little balcony. Without any hesitation, looking like I was supposed to be doing this, I took off my coat, tossed it down to the street below, stood on the balcony rail, caught hold of the bottom railing on Broz's balcony, and chinned myself up. Then I got one hand over the top rail and pulled myself up and over onto his balcony. I wasn't even puffing. The Great Wallenda. I glanced casually down toward the street. Nobody seemed to be gathering. No cops were screaming to a stop, no concerned citizens were pointing up at me. I stood close to the glass door, took out my gun, and banged out the glass around the door catch. Still no hue and cry. Even if there had been, I figured the cops in Georgetown carried fowling pieces and I'd be out of range. I reached through the hole and unlatched the door. Then I carefully pulled my hand back out. You never cut the hand going in, always coming out because you let down. I slid the door open and went in and closed it behind me.

It was the same room. Bed, bureau, desk, beer mug with pencils in it. To my left above a massive Mediterranean-type bureau was a very large mirror framed in ornate mahogany and secured to the wall at all four corners with triangular plastic hasps. I went through one of the bedroom doors into a large green-tiled bathroom with an Italian marble sink set in a mahogany cabinet. Above the sink was another large mirror. There was a door on the opposite side of the bathroom and when I opened it I found another bedroom. I took a quick house tour to make sure I was alone. The bedrooms and connecting bath lay along the front of the building; the building was a big living-dining area and an open kitchen at one end. Normal-sized windows looked uphill away from the river toward Georgetown. The place was ornately furnished in mahogany and expensive carpeting.

I went back to the bathroom and looked at the mirror over the sink. On the right side it was hinged, and I swung it open, ducking under it, and pushed it aside, up against the pebbled-glass tub enclosure. What remained was of course the see-through side of a one-way mirror. It commanded a full view of the bedroom beyond, and anyone who wanted to watch or photograph what went on there had only to do so from here. It was where Ronni Alexander had made her (as far as I knew) videotape debut.

I closed the mirror and looked through the rest of the apartment. I wasn't careful. The broken glass door to the balcony would suggest that apartment security had been violated. I had two purposes: to see what I could find that would be useful, like other videotapes or a picture of Gerry Broz, and also to give the impression that this had been a random burglary. There was no point in making Gerry more careful than I needed to.

There was a wall safe in the apartment. I tried it. It was locked. I didn't give it a second glance. I knew my limitations.

There was nothing else in the apartment that you would be surprised to find in the apartment of an affluent college kid. As far as I could tell, Gerry had no roommate. The lock that had been impenetrable from the outside was easy from the inside. I took about twenty dollars I had found in an old tobacco humidor in loose bills and change, and what appeared to be a small quantity of cocaine, and a pair of diamond cufflinks. Then I left. Outside I walked out onto the bridge and unobtrusively dropped the coke and the cufflinks into the river. The money wasn't incriminating. I kept it to spend at the Market.

Chapter 18

Back at the Market I had a sausage sandwich with fried peppers on French bread and my absolute last cup of coffee for the day. It was my victory lunch, but I was cheating. I knew a lot more than I had before I'd seen the chesty young woman in the HOYAS T-shirt, but I was no closer as far as I could see to solving Alexander's problem.

On the other hand I knew how Broz got the pictures. What I didn't know is how his kid got the pictures. He must be twenty, twenty-one at the most. Ronni Alexander was more than twice his age. Where would their paths cross? What the hell was she doing in his apartment *indelicato*? The forty-six-year-old wife of a U.S. congressman picking up college kids? Possible. If it was true, she'd picked a good one. Talk about luck.

I finished my sandwich and sipped the rest of my final cup of coffee. I looked at my watch, twenty to one. Around eighteen hours till breakfast. Coffee with breakfast was okay. I went back to the Safeway parking lot on Wisconsin, got my rental car, and drove back to the Hay Adams.

From the hotel I called Martin Quirk, who was not in. But Belson was and took the call.

I said, "I'm in Washington, D.C., and I need to know whatever you have on Joe Broz's son Gerald."

He said, "What am I, Travelers Aid?"

I said, "If you will get that for me, when I return I will buy you a case of Rolling Rock Extra Pale beer in the long neck returnable bottles."

"Are you attempting to bribe a law officer?"

"Yes."

"Lemme see what I've got," Belson said. "I'll call you back."

I gave him the number and hung up and stood and looked out the window at the White House. Below, between me and the White House on my side of Pennsylvania Avenue, three busloads of people had unloaded and were demonstrating their support for something in Lafayette Park. I watched them for a while but couldn't figure out what they were demonstrating about and went back to looking at the White House. The mixture of snow and rain and sleet was still falling. I got out the phone book and looked in the Yellow Pages under Restaurants to see if I found one that jogged my memory. While I was doing that Belson called back.

"Gerald Joseph Broz," Belson said. "Born November 18, 1962. Six feet tall, one-ninety-three pounds, black hair, brown eyes, no distinguishing scars or other characteristics. No arrest record. Presently in his senior year at Georgetown University in Washington, D.C. Political science major."

"You got a picture?" I said.

"No."

"He going into the family business when he graduates?"

"Nobody knows. He's the eldest son, the guess is he will, but no way to know. Far as anyone in OCU knows, he's clean."

I said, "Thank you."

"You're welcome. When do I get the beer?"

"Soon as I get back," I said. "You come pretty cheap."

"Cheap?" Belson said. "You fish, you coulda had me for a six-pack."

I hung up and went back to my restaurant listings and found one I remembered and called and made a reservation.

Then I called Wayne Cosgrove at *The Boston Globe* to ask if they had a picture of Gerry Broz. He wasn't in. I looked at my watch. Almost eight hours till I picked up Susan. Time for visions and revisions.

Paragraph six of the gumshoe's manual said when in doubt, follow someone. Paragraph seven said when there is time on your hands, follow someone. I had time on my hands and I didn't know what else to do, so I put on my leather trench coat and my new low-crowned cowboy hat that Susan had bought me for my birthday, and headed back to Georgetown.

The drive back was harder. There was nearly an inch of snow accumulated and Washington was rapidly sinking into hysteria. No school announcements were being broadcast and storm updates were cutting in on the radio every ten minutes. It took me nearly half an hour to get to a meter on M Street, half a block from Gerry Broz's apartment.

At the corner of Thirty-fifth and M, I loitered near the package store, checking my reflection in the window. Actually the cowboy hat Susan had bought me was one of those high-crowned ten-gallon things with a big feather in the band, like Willie Stargell wears. When I had tried it on I hadn't looked like Willie Stargell. I had looked like the Frito Bandito, so we took it back and bought the more modest Gunclub Stetson, with an understated little feather like a trout fly in the band. Susan was after me to get cowboy boots too, but I wasn't ready for them yet. When I got further upscale. Then I could get some, and maybe crossed ammunition belts in the same tone.

As I stood and considered my image a Ford van pulled up in front of Broz's building. It said CANAL GLASS on the side. Two guys got out and removed a large glass sheet from the back and carried the glass into the building. In a couple of minutes I could see them at work on the broken glass door to Broz's balcony. There were no police cars around. I'd bet Broz didn't report it. A kid of Joe Broz's would not be likely to call the cops. He'd either ignore it or turn it over to his father's organization. On the whole I'd prefer he ignored it.

It took the glass-repair crew maybe an hour to take out the old glass and put in the new. In that time nothing else stirred at the apartment. The snow, occasionally mixed with rain, came down, most of it melting, a little bit collecting. Cars coming off Key Bridge were making a continuous high whine as they spun their wheels. The two workmen came down carrying the broken glass panel, slid it into the back of the truck, got in, and skidded away. Above in Broz's apartment all was secure. As I looked the lights went on in the bedroom, stayed on for maybe three minutes, and went off. About a minute later someone emerged from the apartment building. It was a young man with dark hair. He looked about six feet tall and appeared to weigh a soft 190 pounds. He also looked like the male partner in Ronni Alexander's stag film.

It didn't have to be Gerry Broz. There were two other apartments in there, and probably each one housed more than one person. It could be someone else. But it could be him. Paragraph six applied. He headed up Thirty-fifth Street. I followed him.

Where it slants up from the river Thirty-fifth Street is San Franciscan in its ascent. The snow and rain slick that had covered it didn't help matters any. Broz ahead and me behind expended a lot of energy getting up there. We turned left on Prospect, walked two blocks, and there was Georgetown University. Broz went straight to the library and got a stack of bound periodicals out of the stacks and sat in the reading room thumbing through them and taking notes. I couldn't see from where I was what periodicals they were. I nosed about here and there in the reading room and adjacent places. Except at the checkout area, which looked like the security at an airport, there was no one to pay me any attention. Many coeds went about their activities, heedless of my presence. I was not pleased by that.

One of them did pay attention to my subject however. She came in wearing tight jeans and a green vest over a white cable-knit sweater. She sat down opposite my subject and said, "How'd ya do in the poli-sci final, Gerry?"

"I think I aced it," Gerry said. "How about you?"

"I think I knew the stuff, but that bastard Ekkberg hates me."

Gerry shrugged. "Ekky hates everybody, especially girls."

She nodded. They did some more small talk and then

the girl got up and left. Unless the fates were snickering up their sleeve, the kid was Gerry Broz. He even looked like his father, or like his father had. There was a kind of theatricality to him. He sat as if he were being viewed from all sides. But he was softer-looking than his father, not so much overweight as undersinewed, as if he'd walked slowly everywhere he went. He had taken off the tan parka with the dark blue lining he had worn to the library. He was wearing a blue oxford cloth shirt with a buttondown collar and chino pants over Frye boots. His belt was blue with a red stripe running through it and his hair was short and carefully cut. The more I looked at him, the more I was sure it was he in the videotape, and that he was Gerry Broz.

At 6:30 Gerry got up and put on his parka and stowed his notebook in a green book bag and left the library. He allowed them to check the book bag on the way out, and with me discreetly distant he went out into the darkness and walked back to his apartment and went in. I left him there. It was time to get ready for Susan.

Chapter 19

I was dressed to the teeth, dark blue suit and vest with a faint white pinstripe, white silk show hankie, dark red tie with tiny white dots. White broadcloth shirt with a pin collar and French cuffs. My cordovan loafers were shined, I was close shaven, my teeth sparkled. Had the weather been better I'd have worn white flannel trousers and walked upon the beach. Instead I sat beside Susan on a banquette in Rive Gauche and ordered beer.

Susan said "Dewar's and water" to the waiter.

Off to our right there was a family group, obviously mother and father with son and daughter-in-law. The old man was explaining to the son and daughter-in-law what a really world class big deal he was. Occasionally the mother chimed in that yes, he really was a big deal. The son and his wife listened in glum silence, the daughter-in-law forcing a bright smile through it all. Obviously the parents were paying.

There were few other people in the room. The howling

storm had paralyzed Washington as drifts of nearly an inch and a half had piled up along some major arteries.

The waiter brought our drinks.

"Dewar's and water," I said.

"Yes. I don't care really, but everyone at work says if you don't order by name they give you bar whiskey."

I drank a little beer. Molson. Rive Gauche didn't have Rolling Rock Extra Pale either. The All World Big Deal at the next table was telling his kid about how tough you had to be to prevail in business and giving a number of examples of how tough he'd recently been.

"Lonely at the top," I said to Susan.

"But not quiet," Susan said.

"How about I threaten to kill him if he doesn't shut up."

"It would probably work, but the rest of the evening might be a bit strained."

"I know. The world is never simple, is it?"

Susan shrugged. "He's excited by his success. He wants to pass along to his son some of what he knows. He's showing off a little. I'm not sure it's a capital offense."

"He's showing off for the daughter-in-law," I said.

Susan shrugged again, and smiled. "He's male."

The waiter appeared to take our order. I ordered pigeon stuffed with cabbage. Susan ordered sole Veronique. I asked for a wine list. The Big Deal listed some people he'd recently fired. I studied the wine list. Control. If I concentrated on Susan and dinner and wine, I could block the guy out. It was simply a matter of control. The wine steward came by. I ordered Gewurtztramminer. He smiled approvingly, as they always do, took the wine list, and departed.

The Big Deal explained to his son some of the ways the

son could improve professionally. I could feel the muscles bunch a bit behind my shoulders. Susan noticed my shrug to loosen them.

"Getting to you, is he?" she said.

"Takes his work seriously," I said.

"Don't you?"

"Not as seriously as I take you," I said.

The food arrived, and the wine. We were quiet while it was served.

When the servants had departed, Susan said, "Is there an implied criticism there?"

I didn't answer.

"Do you think I take my work more seriously than I take you?"

"At the risk of oversimplification," I said, "yes."

"Because my work has taken me away?"

"In part."

"Your work takes you away. How is that different?"

"When I leave, I leave because I must," I said. "You could have stayed in Boston." Susan started to speak. I made a stop sign with my hand. "It's more than that. You went willingly, you aren't . . ." The more I talked the more churlish it sounded. It wasn't churlish inside. "You aren't sorry. You're having a good time."

"And you'd like it better if I weren't?"

When I had been a small boy someone told me that the blood in your veins was blue, the way it looked through the skin, and that it only turned red when you exposed it to air. What I felt was one thing when I kept it in. It changed color entirely when I exposed it.

"I would like it better if you seemed to be missing me more."

Susan drank some of her wine and put the glass down

very carefully, as if the table were shaky. She looked at the glass for a time, as if it were something she'd suddenly discovered. Then she raised her eyes and looked at me.

"Until I was twenty I was my father's princess, his little JAP. And then I was my husband's wife, the ornament of his career, and after the divorce, not very long after, I met you and became your"—she made a wiffling gesture with her hand—"friend. Always *me* was perceived through *you*— *you* my father, *you* my husband, *you* my friend."

"By whom?" I said. When I was serious my English was good.

"By all of us. By *me* and by *you*, all of *you*. Down here there's no intermediary lens, no *you* through which *me* is seen. Here I am what I am and a great many people are very much taken with me because of what I am and they never even heard of you. Yes, I love that. And yes, I miss you. But missing you is a price I have to pay in order to become completely me. At least for a while. And god-damn it, it's a price I am glad to pay. I sort of expected you'd understand better."

"I kind of hoped I would too," I said. "I'm doing the best I can."

"So," Susan said with emphasis, "am I."

I drank some wine. The truth kept turning to confusion as I tried to speak it. "I think what you're saying I can handle," I said. "But I think you've overcommitted. You are becoming your work. You don't talk the same. You use the jargon of the profession, you drink the drink of the profession, you know who the important people are and get next to them. You've begun to believe in potluck suppers to boost morale. I'm not sure how much you're be-coming *yourself*."

"I'm not becoming myself," Susan said. "I'm trying out

selves, I'm working up a self. That's part of the problem. I never had a center, a core full of self-certainty and conviction. I've merely picked up the colorations of the *yous*: my father, my husband, my . . ."—she smiled a little—". . . friend. Of course I'm becoming more shrink-y than the shrinks. I'm like a kid in her first year at college. And if it helps you any, you might think of me that way, leaving the nest. Even explaining myself limits me, it's intrusive, it compromises me. I want to do what I want to do."

"Unless your supervisor tells you not to," I said.

"That's not fair. It's not . . . it's not even insightful. You still can't get outside your own view. You can't understand someone without a goddamned code. You don't see that for millions of people, male and female, the workplace is the code."

I shook my head. "You have committed yourself to everything I've worked all my life to stay free of."

"I know," Susan said.

"You endorse a way of life I find not only uninviting, I . . . I disapprove of it."

Susan nodded.

"I always assumed," I said, and twiddled with my wineglass as I said it, "I always assumed that someone who found his or her identity the way you're finding yours was . . ."—I spun the stem of the wineglass slowly between my fingers and watched the round bottom circle slowly on the table linen—"shallow."

Susan's gaze on me was steady. "It's a view you tend to impose on anyone close to you. You believe things very strongly. It burdens people."

I nodded. "A person might need to get away from me," I said. "To develop her own views."

I stopped twirling the wineglass and picked it up and

drank some wine. Then I took the wine bottle from the bucket and poured some more into Susan's glass and mine.

"The thing is, you're not shallow," I said. "And if you were, it wouldn't matter. Not only would I follow you into hell. I'd follow you into AT&T."

Susan sampled some of her sole.

"So I was wrong about that," I said. "Makes me wonder what else I was wrong about. Makes me doubt myself. Screws up my autonomy."

I took a bite of my squab. It was delicious. I tried the cabbage; it had a magnificent smoky taste.

"How come I'm still hungry when my heart is breaking?" I said.

Susan smiled. "Old habits are hard to shake," she said.

"The other thing that's killing me," I said, "is, I suppose, a problem of excessive self-concern. But I have offered you what I had always thought was the most desirable thing in the world. I have loved you absolutely, and completely, and without reservation. And I still do. I guess I'm feeling that you are not grateful."

"Good heavens," Susan said. "You're human after all."

"But that's not your problem, is it? That's mine."

"Yes," Susan said. "It would be worth your while to think about whether you love me for my sake or yours."

"I don't want to do that," I said.

"Why not?"

"Everybody needs one pipe dream," I said.

"Love?"

"Romantic love," I said. "I won't give it up."

Chapter 20

I followed Gerry Broz around the next day while Washington dug out from what they seemed to think had been Armageddon. In Boston we would have said the storm missed us. Gerry didn't do anything more remarkable than go to class and then go to the library and then go back to his apartment.

I wandered along behind him and looked at the Georgetown campus. It was a big one, spreading down from the Georgetown Medical Center on Reservoir Road to the low bluff above the river. The older buildings were fieldstone Gothic and the new ones were brick.

In the evening Gerry went up to the library and did more research. While I browsed nearby, three coeds stopped to chat with him. Twice he went outside and smoked a cigarette, and at 9:15 he folded up his notebooks and went back to his apartment. I watched the light in his bedroom window until it went off at 11:30, then I dragged back to the Hay Adams and went to bed exhausted. Sometimes the excitement of an archcriminal is more than a man can manage.

Next morning I was back at it, a thrill a minute. This time we didn't go to class. We strolled briskly down M Street to a coffee shop where Gerry talked with two very young girls, high school age at best, sitting in a booth, for maybe a half hour. Then we set out on a walking tour of Georgetown, stopping at five homes along the way. I noted the address each time. No novice I.

Broz wasn't in any of the homes for more than five minutes. Then he returned briskly to his apartment, opened up the garage, got out a red Datsun 280-Z with a T-roof and headed downtown. I followed him in the rental car. He went straight down Pennsylvania Avenue to the Capitol, around it on one of the circumference roads, and back onto Pennsylvania on the hill, southeast of the Capitol. He parked about two blocks along, got out, and made another series of visits like the ones he'd made in Georgetown. Then he got back into the car and drove to F Street just east of the White House and went into the Old Ebbitt Grill where he had lunch with three other guys his age, one of whom wore a Georgetown warm-up jacket.

The restaurant was narrow and antique-looking, rising three stories, and divided into several small dining rooms. I had a beer and a hamburger at the bar while Gerry and his associates feasted on the next floor up.

When they left, the guy with the warm-up jacket got into the Z with Gerry, and the other two guys followed along behind in a metallic green Mazda sedan. Behind the Mazda, I made three. Back in Georgetown, Gerry put his Z away and the green Mazda parked outside his driveway. The four men went in and I stayed outside.

In about half an hour the two teenage girls I'd seen Gerry breakfasting with showed up and went in. They seemed highly animated when they went in and when they came out around four in the afternoon it was clear that they were drunk. They giggled as they swayed past me up Thirty-fifth Street. I watched them struggle up the incline, and looked back at the apartment and then back at them. They looked like a better bet, paragraph six. I hopped in my car and followed.

Up the hill the two girls separated. One of them kept going and the other turned right down O Street. I turned down O Street behind her.

Half a block down O she stopped to light a cigarette. She was having trouble in the wind when I came up close to her and stopped and got out of the car. She didn't even notice me until I was beside her. She was drunker than she had looked from a distance and kept holding the flame of her lighter two inches to the right of her cigarette. I took it from her and took the cigarette from her mouth and lit it and handed both back to her. I took my wallet from my hip pocket and while I did I let her see the gun on my belt. I opened the wallet, held it toward her, then flipped it closed.

"I'd like to talk to you," I said.

She squinted at me uneasily.

"Get in the car," I said.

"What'd I do?"

"You have the right to remain silent," I said. "You have the right to an attorney. If you cannot afford an attorney, one will be assigned you."

I opened the door. And with a hand on her arm ushered her into the car.

"Anything you say can and will be used against you in a court of law."

I closed the door and went around the car and got in behind the wheel.

"What'd I do?" she said again. She was smoking the cigarette awkwardly, as though she hadn't much experience with it.

I put the car in gear and we rolled slowly along O Street.

"I've got a few questions to ask you," I said.

"I want to see my parents," she said.

"Okay," I said. "We'll go to your home and see them. I'll question you in their presence."

"No," she said.

"Okay then, let's cut the crap. You're drunk in public, you're underage, you've been to a sex orgy, and you're in big trouble."

The part about the orgy was a tribute to invention. Two high school girls with four college boys, drunk in the afternoon, made it a plausible guess. And even if it weren't true, the charge would scare her.

"You got no right to say that to me," she said. But her outrage was weak.

"What's your name?" I was very much the authority figure.

"Linda."

"Linda what?"

She shook her head. I reached over and took her purse.

"You can't do that," she said, and she got much more animated.

I ignored her. Holding the purse between my knees, I fumbled it open with one hand and shuffled through it as I drove.

In her wallet I found a District of Columbia automotive learner's permit that said her name was Linda Remmert and that she was sixteen and a half. I also found a small packet of cocaine.

I looked at her. She had shrunk back in the corner of the seat looking nowhere near sixteen and a half. There were tears on her cheeks. She had close-cut black hair and a slightly uptilted nose. She had obviously begun the day with makeup, but there wasn't much left. I turned left on Wisconsin Avenue without saying anything. I put the cocaine and her learner's permit into my shirt pocket.

"That's not mine," she said.

I didn't say anything.

"It isn't," she said. Her voice was snuffly and the tears continued to trickle down her cheeks.

"Honest to God," she said. "I don't know how it got there."

I kept driving.

"Where we going?" she said.

I shook my head. We drove some more. She had started to cry softly beside me. I felt like a child molester. Sometimes the end justified the means, sometimes it didn't. It seemed to me that lately I was having more trouble sorting out when it did and when it didn't. At the top of the hill on the right was Washington Cathedral. I pulled over in front of it and stopped.

Linda looked at me and tried not to cry.

I turned sideways and leaned my right arm on the back of the seat and said, "Linda, it's going to be all right."

She stared at me blankly.

"What d'ya mean?"

"I mean there's a way out of this for you."

She stared at me and didn't say anything.

"I don't want to put a sixteen-year-old kid in the house of blue lights. I'm after more important stuff. If you'll help me, I'll help you."

"What d'ya want me to do?"

"First I want you to tell me where you got the coke and then I want you to tell me what you were doing in there with Gerry Broz and then we'll go from there."

"I don't want to get no one in trouble," she said.

I nodded. "Least of all you," I said. "Listen, honey, I gotta have something out of this. I don't want it to be you, so give me somebody else. Somebody that deserves it more."

Chapter 21

In twenty minutes I had it all.

Gerry Broz dealt coke. If you didn't have money for coke, he'd trade for sex.

"If he thought you were sexy," Linda said with pride.

"For himself?"

"For himself and his friends," Linda said.

"If they thought you were sexy."

Linda nodded. Broz also dealt among many of the Washington fashionables, Linda said. She didn't know who, but Gerry bragged of the people he sold to.

"Or traded with," I said.

"Not just kids," Linda said. "Grownups, middle-aged women."

"How do you know?"

"They have parties, granny parties they call them. Gerry calls the older women grannies. They let us come and watch."

"Watch?"

Linda nodded. She thought it was neat.

"They have a way to peek. In the bathroom there's a one-way mirror. You can watch."

It was obviously the most interesting thing Linda did and she liked to talk about it once she got going. It was as if she'd forgotten why I was asking. She was an excited teenage girl telling about her adventures, except her speech was slurring while she talked.

"Sonofagun," I said. "I'd like to see that."

Linda nodded. "It's really bogus," she said. "Some of those women, really high-class women." She shook her head at the bogusness of it all.

"Could you sneak me in?" I said.

Her eyes widened.

"I'll bet you could," I said. "You sneak me in and you're home free. It'll be like I never saw you. I give you back the coke and the learner's permit as soon as we're out."

Linda said, "I don't know."

I said, "I'll bet you could. You can go right in the front door and through the living room and into the bathroom. If everything's happening in the bedroom, there's no way they'd see you."

Linda was silent. "Yeah, that's . . . How do you know what the place looks like?"

"There's not much I don't know," I said. "Keep it in mind." Delphic.

"I don't know."

"When's the next, ah, performance?" I said.

"Tomorrow morning," she said. "Eleven o'clock."

"The early bird catches the worm," I said. "I'll pick you up right here at ten of eleven. We'll slip right on in."

"Okay. I guess. I mean, what if I say no?"

I smiled at her without warmth. Every year it got easier

to smile without warmth. I was starting to feel like Jimmy Carter.

"Well, how will we do it?"

"You'll go in," I said. "Then when the action gets under way, you'll come and get me."

"I usually watch with my friend. What if she says something?"

"Tell her not to. Tell her I'm your dad and I believe in togetherness. That's your problem."

"You're older than my dad," she said.

"Maybe not, maybe I've just had a harder life."

She giggled a little and hiccuped. "Not unless you've been married to my mother," she said.

I let that pass. I didn't ask how old her father was. I was afraid to.

"Margy's okay," Linda said. "She'll keep quiet."

I took the cocaine and her learner's permit from my shirt pocket.

"Remember," I said. "I have you locked, if I want to press it."

She nodded.

"Don't get smart when the booze wears off," I said. "Don't think I'm too swell a person to bust you."

She shook her head vigorously. More vigorously than I liked. I drove her to the corner of her street and let her out.

"Here, tomorrow," I said. "Ten of eleven."

"Yes," she said, and got out and walked away from me fast without looking back.

Chapter 22

Susan and I were having a drink in The Class Reunion on H Street. The place was full of journalists and booze was at flood tide.

"An orgy?"

I nodded.

"You have a date with a sixteen-year-old girl to go watch an orgy?"

I nodded again.

"And you got the date how?"

"By impersonating a police officer," I said.

Susan nodded. She drank a small swallow of Dewar's and water.

"Do you plan to participate?" she said.

"Not unless you turn up there."

Susan nodded and kept nodding. "At a—what did the little dear call it?"

"A granny party."

"Yes, a granny party."

"Well, they're not really grannies," I said. "The kids are so young, that's all. They just say that."

Susan nodded again. I poured some Budweiser from the bottle.

"I didn't order by name," I said. "Wonder if this is the house beer."

Susan ignored me.

"What do you expect to find?" she said.

"Same old thing," I said. "I won't know till I look. I just keep pushing and looking. Better than sitting and waiting."

"It requires a rather considerable negative capability," Susan said.

"Lots of things do," I said.

"Want to walk?" she said. "I don't get enough exercise down here."

"Sure."

I paid for the drinks and we left. It was a fine night. Temperature in the fifties, clear. At the corner of H Street we turned east, toward the White House on Pennsylvania Avenue.

"Do you think Alexander would really drop out of the race rather than expose his wife?"

"Absolutely," I said.

"It would be hard to choose otherwise," Susan said. "Be hard to avoid feeling guilty."

"Yes, it would," I said. "But I think he is better than that. I think he doesn't want her hurt."

"If he dropped out," Susan said, "he could feel virtuous and make her feel guilty."

"He says he doesn't want her ever to know that he even knows about the films."

"It would allow him to feel superior to her," Susan said.

We walked by the enormous granite pile of the Executive Office Building next to the White House, across from Blair House. It was everything an executive office building should be.

"You shrinks are so cynical," I said. "Is there any behavior that is not self-serving?"

Susan was silent for a bit as we walked along in front of the White House.

"Probably not," Susan said.

"So that the woman who dies trying to save her child does so because if she didn't she couldn't live with herself?"

"Something like that. People will do a great deal to support the image they have of themselves."

"Hard to be romantic seeing life that way," I said.

Susan shrugged.

"Doesn't allow you to believe in heroes or villains or good or bad, does it?" I said. "If all actions are selfish."

"Heroes and villains, good and bad, are not applicable in my work."

"Grant that," I said. "But mightn't they be applicable in your life? How do you know how to act?"

We turned down along the east side of the White House.

"Of course I have vestiges of my upbringing, and religious training, and school inculcation that nag me under the heading of conscience. But consciously and rationally I try to do what serves me most at least cost to others."

"And when there's a conflict?"

"I try to resolve it."

The White House was brightly lit from all sides inside the iron fence that surrounds it. There must have been security apparatus, but I didn't see much. We turned left on Pennsylvania again.

"You don't understand, do you?" Susan said.

"Seems pretty Hobbesian to me," I said.

"Despite the fact that I have much more formal education than you do, and despite your somewhat physical approach to problem solving, you are an intellectual and I am not. You speculate on questions just like this one—how does one determine his behavior. You read Hobbes and God knows who else. I don't even know Hobbes's first name."

"Thomas," I said.

"Or what he said, or when. The kinds of questions about how to act that you are asking rarely come up for me, or the people in my work. We are results-oriented."

"They come up quite often," I said, "in my work."

"Of course they do. Partly because it's you that is doing the work, and partly because you've chosen a kind of work where those questions will come up."

The august march of government architecture reared on either side of us, the Federal Energy Administration, the Post Office Building, the Justice Department, and across the street the FBI Building. My knee started to bend in genuflection before I caught myself. The municipal neoclassicism of the architecture was a little silly, but on the other hand it looked the way it ought to. What would have been less silly?

"Can you analyze our relationship in the light of Silvermanian pragmatism?" I said.

"I love you because I find it compelling to be loved so entirely. You love me because as long as you do you can believe in romantic love."

Ahead on the right was the National Gallery with its new wing. Beyond rose the Capitol, on its hill.

We turned back up Pennsylvania Avenue.

"Too bad it's so late," I said. "If it were still daytime, we could take the FBI tour and maybe they'd show me a tommy gun."

"That's your closing comment?" Susan said.

"I have no closing comment," I said.

"What do you think of what I have been saying?"

"I think it is bullshit," I said.

"Would you care to support that view?"

"No," I said.

Chapter 23

Linda was there at ten of eleven. Without any booze in her she looked tight and pinched and scared and embarrassed and shy and as restless as a willow in a windstorm.

I smiled when she got into the car.

"I hope I'm dressed okay," I said. "I've never been to a granny party before."

Linda didn't speak. She looked straight ahead. As I slid away from the curb I said, "We need a plan."

She nodded.

"Who'll be there?" I said.

"Me and Margy," she said. "And Jerry and Butch and Claude and Jimmy and the two grannies."

"And *moi*," I said.

She nodded.

"Who'll be watching through the one-way mirror?"

"Just me and Margy."

"Okay," I said. "I'll wait outside. You and Margy go ahead and get comfortable in the bathroom. Then when the four men and the two ladies get to it, you go out through the other bedroom and around through the living room and open the apartment door.

"What if they catch me?"

"I'll protect you."

"Against four guys?"

I made a muscle in my upper arm. "My strength, little lady, is as the strength of ten."

"And you have a gun," she said.

I shrugged. "That's part of it," I said.

"How come there's no other cops with you? Don't you have any back-up?"

Everybody watches television.

"If I had back-up, honey, I couldn't cover up for you."

She nodded and looked at me for the first time.

"You really are going to let me off, aren't you?"

"Yes," I said. "I am."

We stopped on M Street in sight of Gerry's building. I looked up at the apartment windows. "The window in the bathroom is blacked out, for the one-way mirror. The last windows on top there must be the spare bedroom."

Linda said, "Yes."

"After you open the door for me, open the bedroom window. I'll see it and come up."

"Okay."

We sat quietly. Linda was pale. Her swallowing was audible. Two well-dressed women in maybe their early forties walked past up on M Street and turned into the building. The grannies? In another minute Linda said in a strained voice, "There's Margy."

"Okay," I said. "Go to it."

Linda looked condemned as she got out of the car. But she went, passively. She fell in beside Margy, and as they talked Margy glanced back once, toward the car, and then nodded, and together she and Linda went into the apartment.

At 11:15 three college boys came down the hill on Thirty-fifth Street and went into Gerry's building. I took a Polaroid camera out of the Speedo gym bag I used to carry gear in. Casey, Crime Photographer. It was almost noon when I saw the bedroom window go up. I got out of the car and walked across the street into the apartment building. I had no more trouble with the outside door than I had the last time.

At the third floor the front door to Gerry Broz's apartment was open a crack. I pushed it open. There were faint sounds of rock music in the apartment. I walked the length of the living room, past the dining nook, and into the spare bedroom. The bathroom door was closed. I opened it. The two girls stood half-watching through the one-way mirror, half-looking for me. The sound of rock music was a little louder, but still very muffled. He must have soundproofed the bedroom. Margy had red hair done in a long braid. I smiled politely and gestured both girls away from the window. They edged back against the rear wall of the bathroom, afraid, but excited too. They looked at everything I did.

I looked through the mirror. The two well-dressed women I'd seen earlier were there, only they weren't well dressed anymore. They were both naked. So were the four college boys.

The women looked naked, in a way that women never do in skin magazines. These women were real, with the fine roughening of skin here and there, the tiny sag at the breast, the small folds across the stomach that real women, and men, have. It made them more, rather than less, seductive, I thought, because it emphasized their nakedness, and in a sense their vulnerability. It also made me feel a little sadder for them. That kind of vulnerability shouldn't be handed around. It was for someone who loved you and was vulnerable too.

I began to take pictures through the mirror as the four boys and two women engaged rather raucously in group sex. I made sure that I got at least one full-face shot of all the participants, and enough of the larger scene so that it was clear what was going on.

It took me no more than ten minutes and when I was through there was a great deal more still going on behind the mirror. I had what I'd come for. I smiled at the two girls and took the learner's permit and the coke from my pocket and gave both to Linda. Her eyes widened as she took them.

I said softly, "I can still cause you a lot of grief, my love, if you or Margy were to rat on me."

They both nodded.

"Enjoy," I said, and walked out with my pictures.

At 4:12, when the two once-again well-dressed women came out of the apartment, I was waiting for them, with the car headed in the direction they'd come from, into town on M Street. A block and a half down they got into a silver-gray Subaru wagon and drove toward Wisconsin Avenue. I followed them. It had worked so well with Linda I thought I'd try it again. I was beginning to have a plan.

Chapter 24

The Subaru dropped a passenger on P Street and continued on for three more blocks. At random I decided to stick with the driver. It would be harder for her to claim she was dragged against her will. She pulled into the driveway of a handsome brick-front town house. The brick was painted an antique white and there was a bow window to the right of the entrance with the wood trim painted Williamsburg blue.

I pulled in next to the curb and got out and joined her at the door.

"Excuse me," I said, "but we need to talk."

She was a little under the influence, and she looked frightened at being braced by a stranger at her doorway. I held out a picture of her, recently taken, and said, "I mean you no harm. I just want to talk."

She looked at the picture. "Jesus Christ," she said.

"Yes," I said. "I agree."

"Where did you . . . ?"

"We need to talk. We can sit in my car if you wish, or walk on the street if you'd feel safer, or go in your house."

"What do you want?"

She had olive skin and blond hair. Her cheekbones were high and her dark eyes were almond-shaped. There were pleasant crow's feet at the corners of her eyes.

"Want to walk?" I said. I still held the picture so that she could see it. As she looked at it a faint flush tinged her skin. Embarrassment. A good sign.

She nodded and we descended her front steps and walked east along her street.

"Are you going to blackmail me?" she said.

"In a sense, yes," I said. "May I see your driver's license?"

"I . . ."

"I merely wish to know your name. I'll give it back. If you won't show it to me, it's all right. I'll get your name anyway. I know your address and the registration number of your car."

"Then why don't you just ask me my name?"

"Because I'd have no way to know if you'd given me the right name without checking anyway. Your license will save me that trouble."

"What if I tell you to go to hell?" she said.

"I'll make the pictures public."

"I'm not ashamed," she said.

"I'm not telling you you should be," I said. "But do you want the pictures public?"

She was silent as we walked. I could sense her fighting to get lucid. Finally she stopped and turned and looked directly at me.

"No," she said.

"License please," I said.

She took a wallet from her purse, and the license from the wallet and gave it to me. Her name was Cynthia Knox.

"Thank you, Cynthia. What I need is information."

"No money?"

I shook my head. "What I want is information about Gerry Broz."

"You're not a policeman?"

"No."

She looked puzzled. "What do you want to know?"

"How'd you meet him?"

She gave a short, joyless laugh. "Actually I met him through my husband."

"How does your husband know him?"

"He . . . he just knows him."

"What's your husband do?"

She hesitated.

"I can find it out," I said. "I could even hang around your house until he came home and ask him."

She shook her head. Her dark eyes looked a little clearer. "You really aren't a cop?"

"No."

She sighed. "Cocaine," she said. "My husband used to score coke from him."

"And what does your husband do?"

"He's with the Department of Transportation."

"How'd he meet Gerry?"

"A friend that teaches at Georgetown."

"What could be more natural?" I said.

"Coke's a fact of life in D.C.," she said.

"How about the woman that was with you today?"

"I don't think I should tell you about someone else."

"Same old answer. I can find out. I know where she lives. I know what she looks like. I have her picture too."

"I still don't feel right."

"Don't use her name," I said. "How'd she meet Gerry?"

"I introduced her."

"He the candyman for her family too?"

Cynthia nodded. "I think so."

"You recruit her for the, ah, matinees?"

Cynthia said, "Yes," very softly.

"Do you know how many other women party like that with Gerry?"

"No."

"Do you know if there are others?"

"Yes. There are. Sometimes there have been other women there. I don't know them."

"Always the same young men?"

"No. Always Gerry, but the others change. Sometimes Gerry doesn't even participate. How did you get that picture?"

"I stood in the bathroom and took it through the one-way mirror. That's what Gerry does when he's not participating. Only he uses videotape."

Cynthia stopped dead still and looked at me.

All the houses on Cynthia's street were brick with colonial trim. Very elegant, very muted. Softened by care and charm and maybe a faint scent of the river that drifted up.

"Videotape?"

I nodded. "Yes. I represent someone who was video-taped."

"My God."

"Your friend's husband with the government?"

She nodded. Her mouth opened and closed. Wordless.

We turned back toward her house. The trees along the street were old trees, maples mostly, and even leafless in December they looked graceful and sheltering. Cynthia looked at her watch.

"My husband will be home in an hour and a half," she said.

We walked some more.

"Can we sit in your car for a little while?" Cynthia said.

"Sure."

We were silent till we got to the rental and sat.

"What are you going to do?" she said.

"I'm going to try and put Gerry out of business without blowing the whistle on the person I represent, or anyone else."

"Can you do that?"

"Maybe."

It was nearly dark. We were getting close to the winter solstice.

"Have you ever watched the way politicians' wives look at them with an adoring smile in all their public appearances?" Cynthia said.

"Yeah."

"I've been doing that in public for nineteen years," she said. "And my husband's not even a politician. He's a bureaucrat."

I nodded. I'm not sure in the dark that she could see me. It didn't matter. I didn't think she was really talking to me.

"Nineteen years breathless with adoration. At all the parties we could get invited to, and when we weren't invited he'd be in dark despair and I'd have to cheer him up adoringly. Even when he was at work I had to adore him from afar at bridge games and luncheons among department wives and charity teas. The perfect complement to him. The adornment of his career. The beautiful wife, the lovely children, the gracious home."

"Kids still home?" I said.

"No. Private school. See them on holidays. A fine school in Virginia. One of the assistant secretaries sends his daughter there."

Two young girls in school uniforms walked past. They looked Indian or perhaps Pakistani. Their skirts were the identical blue plaid. They wore blue knee socks and blue blazers over white blouses. One wore cowboy boots, the other wooden clogs with a leather slip-on top. Diversity.

"Some women drink," she said. "I do gangbangs."

"With college kids," I said.

"I am as old as their mothers."

"Do a little dope with them too, I imagine."

She nodded. She was watching the two schoolgirls as they diminished down the narrowing perspective of the long residential street.

"I've already had hot flashes," she said, watching the schoolgirls. "Imagine that? Hot flashes. Pretty soon a mustache and middle-aged hump. You know what the kids call us?"

"Grannies," I said. "This morning you attended a granny party."

She nodded. The schoolgirls were quite small in the distance now. She shook her head.

"When I was a little girl there was a song my father used to sing to me," she said. "One line in it was 'Stay away from college boys, when you're on a spree/Take good care of yourself, you belong to me.'" She sang the line over again and her voice was a little shaky. The street-lights had gone on and in the gleam of the one nearest us I could see the brightness of tears on her face.

"Nothing is irredeemable," I said.

"I don't even know why I do it," she said. "Neither does Ellie. There's some thrill to it, but mostly it's humiliating. The boys are crude and stupid. Afterward I feel like . . . like something that's been passed around."

"That's part of its charm," I said.

The schoolgirls turned a corner, far down the street, and disappeared. Cynthia looked at me. Her face was wet.

"Charm?"

"Sure. You're acting out a lot of stuff that I'm not qualified to analyze, but you've found a way to do it and build in your own punishment."

She stared at me for a long time. "You think I need a shrink?"

I shrugged. "What you're doing doesn't seem to please you. Maybe a shrink. Maybe a divorce? Maybe a boy-friend on the side? Maybe a job?"

"I think psychology is a lot of crap," she said.

"Okay by me," I said. "All I'm saying is that if you're unhappy, there are other solutions besides balling a bunch of dim-witted college kids."

She nodded slowly. "I've got to go in," she said. "My husband will be home."

"I'll keep you out of it," I said. "I might ask you to write out a statement of what you told me that I could show to a private person. But I probably won't need it."

I took the picture of her from my shirt pocket and gave it to her. "It's the only one I took that shows your face," I said.

She took it. "Do you think there's videotape?"

"If there is, I'll take care of it," I said.

"Why do this for me?"

"I'm doing it for the person I represent," I said. "Costs me nothing to include you."

"And Ellie?"

"Sure."

She got out of the car and stood for a moment on the sidewalk. I got out on my side and leaned my forearms on the roof and looked at her.

"It's really odd," she said. "I don't even know your name and you know things about me that I've never told anyone."

"As they used to say in the movies, your secret is safe with me."

She took a step toward her house and hesitated; she looked back at me. "Is it going to be all right?"

"Sure," I said. "But stay away from college boys, when you're on a spree."

She nodded and took two more steps and stopped again.

"Thank you," she said.

"You're welcome."

She reached her front steps and turned at her front door and looked at me.

"Mrs. Knox." I said. "For what it's worth, I think you're quite beautiful."

She stayed motionless at her door for a moment, looking back at me. Then she opened it and went in.

Chapter 25

I spent most of the next day calling on people that Gerry Broz had called on in the aftermath of the great blizzard. I'd made note of the addresses and now I went visiting— Georgetown in the morning, Capitol hill in the afternoon. Some people weren't home, many of the people that were home wouldn't talk with me, but I made progress. Enough.

My approach was open and honest. Like my face.

"This is off the record," I told an elegant young woman in a town house on Fourth Street. "I'm doing work for a government agency. I won't mention the name, but it's a three-letter agency."

She stood in her open door in a silk lounging outfit and nodded. Her hair was black with a good-looking sprinkle of premature silver.

"You don't have to even give your name, and you're free to deny anything you say. I'm looking for background only."

She nodded again. Her dark eyes were enlarged by an enormous pair of glasses with jade-green rims.

"There is a young man who sells cocaine to you, and to many of your neighbors, good people, not criminals. He is covertly connected," I said, "to a foreign power with interests antithetical to those of the United States."

"I don't know anything about it," she said.

I shook my head impatiently, but friendly. "No, no. We don't care about the cocaine. I'll snort a little myself on weekends. We've got bigger fish to fry."

"What do you want?" she said.

"The name he's using," I said. "We haven't been able to establish his cover name, and we don't want to risk tipping him to our interest. All I want from you is his name."

She frowned. I was wearing my suit and a clean shirt and trying like hell to look like someone who had gone to Yale and worked now for a three-letter government agency. I smiled sincerely, encouragingly. You can trust your government.

"You needn't admit anything about any proscribed substance," I said. "Merely a name."

"I . . ." She shook her head.

"I guess all of us are cynical now," I said. "I guess that there's no point talking about duty, about patriotism. I guess it's too late for that kind of talk. But I must say that you have a chance here, at no cost to yourself, to do your country a service."

I looked directly at her, standing straight.

"Gerry Broz," she said. "That's the name he uses here."

"Thank you very much," I said. "We will not bother you again. You have my word." I put out my hand, she took it. We shook, and I went on down Fourth Street to where I'd parked the car.

I replayed that scene maybe twenty times that day. In two other instances I got the name. Everyone else told me to beat it. Whatever happened to duty, honor, country? But I had enough. None of it would stand up in court, but I wasn't going to court. I was building evidence for a different forum.

At the sixteenth house I picked up a tail. It wasn't amateurish, but it wasn't Bulldog Drummond either. Two guys in jackets and ties, driving a dark blue Chevy sedan with District plates on it. One of them wore sunglasses. They stayed behind me for the rest of the afternoon. They followed me back to the Hay Adams. When I gave my car to the doorman they moved on down Sixteenth Street, and when I came out half an hour later showered and reshaved and damned near preppy in my Harris tweed jacket, they were gone.

I guessed that someone I'd talked to had called Gerry Broz and Gerry had called someone and they had sent out two employees to take a look. Unless they were even clumsier than their tail job suggested, they'd be able to get my name by tracing the plate numbers to the car rental company. Then they'd check at the hotel and establish that I stayed there.

Then they'd call in and report to whoever sent them and whoever sent them would probably call Gerry and then they'd decide what to do about it. There wasn't much for me to do but go about my business. At least I had stirred up some activity. I'd worry about their next move when they made it. Readiness is all.

My business at the moment was to pick Susan up at work and drive her out Wisconsin Avenue to the Mazza Mall in Chevy Chase. I picked her up at 5:30. She was standing out front in the early evening. Looking at her made me wonder if some of her patients got better just by staring.

"A deal is a deal," I said. "I shop with you tonight, and Saturday you go with me to the National Gallery."

"Yes," she said, "but no big sighs and stifled yawns while I'm in here. I need to concentrate completely."

"And when it's over we eat and drink," I said.

"Shopping is never over," Susan said. "It is merely suspended."

The Mazza Mall was Rodeo Drive compressed and three stories high. The architecture was L.A., or maybe Dallas, opulent with a big Neiman-Marcus branch anchoring one end of the building. Susan had a charge at Neiman-Marcus and headed directly there. To say that Susan shopped would be like saying that sharks eat. It was disciplined frenzy. While she was at it I kept close watch on the clientele, which was multinational and very stylish and almost entirely female. By actual count, women in the Mazza Mall preferred pants to skirts by a four to one margin and preferred the pants very snug over the backside in nearly every case.

The mall closed finally for the night and we left, Susan still gleaming with a hunter's fierce intensity, me less so.

Outside the mall, slightly east of it and across Wisconsin Avenue, was a familiar restaurant front. My heart leapt up.

"My God, Suze, there's a Hamburger Hamlet."

Susan nodded.

"There's one in Chicago too," I said.

"Would you care to go into this one and eat something? I'll bet I can guess the house specialty."

"It's one of my favorites," I said. "There are many of them in L.A., but I didn't know they were creeping east."

"Isn't this thrilling?" Susan said.

"Ah, Suze," I said, "that world-weary pose ill becomes you. Come on, you'll see."

We went into the Hamburger Hamlet and settled in a red leather booth (well, maybe red vinyl) and I ordered beer and Susan had a glass of white wine. The beer came in an enormous schooner. It made me smile just to look at it.

"Ah," Susan said, "I begin to understand your enthusiasm."

Susan's purchases were stacked on the seat around her and some on my side. She rarely wore the same thing twice in my memory, and back in the house in Smithfield her clothes were in every closet.

"Lucky we found this shopping mall," I said. "You'd probably have had to go to work naked."

She smiled at me. "Even I wonder now and then about myself," she said.

"How the hell do you afford it?" I said. "Being a predoctoral intern isn't a get-rich-quick scheme."

"Alimony," she said.

"How the hell can you be liberated and accept alimony?" I said.

Again the smile, innocent, beautiful, glorious, and satanic. "Exploit the oppressor," she said.

The waiter brought us our supper, a large cheeseburger for me, a smaller cheeseburger for Suze, two salads, and another schooner of beer.

"How is your case?"

"It might work out," I said. "I know Joe Broz's kid Gerry made the tapes of Ronni Alexander. I know he deals cocaine to a variety of D.C.'s better citizens. I have some names of some of them and their tacit admission. I know that Gerry trades coke for sex among some teenyboppers, and I know he runs what he calls granny parties for his college chums and a select circle of bored, and/or neurotic housewives."

"What good does all that do you?" Susan said.

"Well, I know how Joe got the tapes. And I'm beginning to think about how to get them back. I can, after all, put a lot of pressure on his kid."

"Isn't that dangerous?" Susan said.

I took a long pull on the beer. "Man's afraid to die's afraid to live," I said.

"That's simple bullshit," Susan said.

"Oh, you noticed that too, huh?"

"It will be dangerous, won't it?"

"Maybe," I said. "I don't know. I'm not exactly clear on how much Joe's involved with this. It just doesn't have his tone. It's too complicated. Too clever. Joe started out breaking people's kneecaps with a baseball bat. He never got much more subtle than that."

"Well, what do you think is going on?"

"I don't know. I just know that all this isn't Joe's style."

"Maybe the boy is acting on his own," Susan said.

"Except that his father's organization is involved. Vinnie Morris came and talked with me."

"Who's he?"

"He's the, ah, executive officer."

"Uh-huh."

"And then the hooligans in Springfield, and Louis Nolan."

She nodded. "Would they do things for the boy without involving the father?"

I shrugged. "Maybe, down the line, if they thought it came from Joe . . . but Vinnie." I shook my head. "Vinnie would know whether it came from Joe or not."

"So how will you find out?"

"Eventually I'm going to have to talk with Joe," I said. "But not until after Saturday. I'm not going back to Boston until we even up."

"My Mazza Mall for your National Gallery," Susan said. Her face was as it had always been: intricate, beautiful, expressive. In the last year somehow it had also become faintly remote, as if always she were listening to a whisper, barely audible, from someplace else: her name, maybe, tiny and hushed. Susan, Susan, Susan.

Chapter 26

The blue Chevy was behind me the next morning when Susan and I left the hotel, and it was still behind us when I dropped her off at work. They tailed more aggressively this time, like they didn't care if I spotted them. That meant, probably, that when they got a chance they were going to accost me. I decided to give them the chance.

I went down North Capitol Street and around the Capitol and parked on Madison Drive in the mall down by the new National Gallery annex. It was early and the tourists hadn't taken all the spots yet. Behind me at the curb along the reflecting pool in front of the Capitol the souvenir wagons were already in place selling snack food and pennants and ashtrays and paperweights and T-shirts and booklets and maps and hats and Sno-Kones and postcards and key fobs and oversized ballpoint pens, and everything except maybe the food had the name WASHINGTON, D.C. on it. The early bird catches the worm.

I got out of the car and leaned against the hood while

the tail got itself parked and the two neat guys in their ties and jackets got out and walked over to me. They looked like the kind of guys you see playing doubles at your tennis club. Tallish, huskyish, blandish. One of them had a neat blond mustache. Their hair was short in back and long on the sides, fringing over their ears. The guy without the mustache wore sunglasses with gold wire rims. He had a long oval face and seemed to have cut his chin shaving that morning. The guy with the mustache showed no sign of cutting himself. He was probably the agile one.

I smiled at them as they walked over to me.

The one with the sunglasses said, "Is your name Spenser?"

I said, "Yes, it is, and let me tell you, it's damned nice to be recognized."

"Congressman Browne would like you to stop around to his office this morning, if it's convenient."

"A congressman? Little old me?"

The guy with the sunglasses nodded wearily. His pal, the well-coordinated one without the razor nick, stood a little to my left as we talked and clasped his hands behind his back. He was being impassive.

I said, "Is the congressman an early riser?"

"I beg your pardon?"

"Will he be in yet?" I said.

"Oh. Yes. Shall we go now?"

"Sure."

"It will be easier if you ride with us. They won't let you park up on the hill without a sticker."

"Okay. Can you fix it if I get tagged down here for parking?"

The impassive one said, "Ignore it. The fucking district government will lose the ticket eight times out of ten."

Still waters run deep. I got into the car and we whisked up the hill. The impassive one drove and when we got to the Cannon Office Building on Independence he stayed with the car and the guy with the sunglasses took me in.

We began, of course, with the inevitable rotunda. There was a cop with a gun sitting at a desk, but he didn't pay us any attention and we went right on past and down a corridor.

The Cannon House Office Building was not entirely harmonious. The halls were quite elegantly tiled in white and gray marble. The walls were done in welfare-office green wallboard. From the ceiling of the corridor hung light fixtures, the ugly utilitarian bulbs concealed by large, textured globes that looked sort of like misshapen white pineapples. My host moved briskly along the first floor corridor. The representative from North Carolina had both a state and an American flag posted outside his office. We passed Meade Alexander's office, no flags. How patriotic was that? The corridor was full of young preppy-looking women, congressional staff, bustling about, tending to the nation's needs. A pork barrel to be shared, a log to be rolled, in quest of more perfect union.

Browne's office was between Shannon of Massachusetts and Roukema of New Jersey. Or more precisely it was between Roukema Annex, and Roukema, but I was counting congresspersons, not offices, and they were the ones on each side of Bobby Browne. Outside it said REPRESEN-TATIVE ROBERT P. BROWNE, COMMONWEALTH OF MASSACHU-SETTS. There was a state seal on the door below his name. We went in.

The office was a reception and work area. Three young women were in it. Two wore white blouses with Peter Pan collars. The other wore an open-necked man-tailored pink shirt with a buttondown collar. Over it she wore a cable-stitched green cardigan sweater. You usually don't see a cardigan sweater except at golf matches and rescue missions. Maybe they weren't cardigans when worn by women. On the walls were pictures of Browne and several presidents.

"The congressman in?" my host said. He spoke briskly too.

"Yes, Barry. He said for you and . . . He said go right in."

We went into the inner office. And there he was. Silver-haired, long-faced, and tanned. He stood when we came in and he was a good two inches taller than I was. Six three at least. His hands were long and narrow and his fingers looked as if they'd do intricate work well. He had on a double-breasted gray flannel suit, pink shirt, red tie, and pink show hankie.

"Morning, Barry," he said. "It seems you were successful."

Barry nodded me toward a chair.

"And good morning to you, Mr."—his eyes flicked down at his desk and back up at me—"Spenser. Thank you very much for coming by so promptly."

I sat in the chair Barry had indicated.

"Barry," Browne said, "I don't think I'll be needing you just now. Thanks very much. Check in with me later perhaps."

Barry nodded and said he would and walked briskly out. Nobody in D.C. was spinning his wheels. There was probably a boon to be doggled and Barry was anxious to get to it.

When he left and the door was closed Browne sat back down in his chair and let it tip back and put his feet up on the desk and clasped his hands behind his head.

We looked at each other like that for a while. His chair was on a swivel. Mine wasn't. I wanted to out-casual him, but tipping over backward in a straight chair would probably hurt more than help. I sat straight but comfortable, folded my hands in my lap, and smiled at him winningly. Browne nodded his head slightly, smiling a small smile of his own.

The office was paneled in mahogany and behind Browne's desk was an American flag and one bearing the insignia of the commonwealth. The mahogany wasn't real, it was plywood, grooved and colored. Probably why he wanted to run for the Senate. A senator probably got real mahogany. Between the flags on the wall hung a picture of Franklin Roosevelt.

"I guess the best approach to this, Mr. Spenser, is to be straight. You have been going around asking questions about a young man whose family is from my district. The questions are rather incriminating. You have also been impersonating a federal, ah, person."

I nodded. My smile got more winning. I leaned forward a little so I could gaze more fully and openly into Browne's pale blue eyes.

"Naturally we looked into you."

"Of course," I said.

"Some of my people back in the district gave me quite a full report on you, on your occupation, your reputation"—he waved a hand vaguely—"all of that."

"Yes," I said.

Browne pursed his lips and nodded his head some more. The picture of Roosevelt must have been taken before the war. He looked full-faced and clear-eyed.

Brown ran his tongue over his upper teeth without

opening his mouth. "Well," he said, "I didn't get here by being afraid to speak out. Do you have proof to substantiate your charges against Gerry Broz?"

"Proof is something you decide in court, Congressperson. What you mean is evidence."

Browne looked a little less relaxed. But the art of the possible was his line. "I stand corrected," he said. "Do you have evidence?"

I said, "Um-hmm."

He pursed his lips again and moved his tongue around behind them. "What have you?" he said.

"The goods. The smoking pistol. Take your choice."

"Don't be evasive."

I smiled sincerely. "I will if I want to," I said.

Browne took his hands from where they were clasped behind his head and folded them across his chest.

"All right," he said. "Enough. I am a U.S. congressman and I've been here a long time and I've got one hell of a big clout around here. You are about to get yourself in trouble that's deep, wide, and permanent."

"If the walls were real mahogany," I said, "I'd probably buckle. But . . ." I spread my hands.

Browne was getting mad, and trying not to let it show, and not succeeding. "Do you, by any chance, know who that young man's father is?"

I nodded.

"Then perhaps you have some idea of the kind of pressure he can bring to bear, in case mine is not enough."

"There's no in-case to it, Congressperson. Yours is not enough."

"I am not going to argue with you, Spenser. I want you to stay away from Gerry Broz. You've been warned. If you persist, let it be on your head."

"Does Joe know about Gerry?" I said.

"Know what? How would I know what Gerry Broz's father knows? What kind of a question is that?"

"One I think I can answer," I said. "If Joe knew, then Gerry would have gone to him, not you, and some people that might be able to do damage would have showed up, not those two computer salesmen you sent."

Browne was deciding to stonewall it. He stared at me with his face empty. Probably his only genuine look.

I shook my head. "Joe doesn't know," I said.

Browne kept looking at me. Behind the empty look was fear. This wasn't how he'd wanted it to go.

"Who called this meeting anyway?" I said.

"Enough," he said. "It is over. Good day, sir."

I stood. "Good day, Congressperson," I said.

He stood up suddenly. "I am not a goddamned congressperson," he said. His voice was raspy. "I am a congress*man*, goddamn it, congress*man*."

I stopped at his door and halfway out leaned back in.

"We are all God's persons," I said.

Chapter 27

Susan and I spent all day Saturday at the National Gallery. We looked at the special Rodin exhibit and we cruised through the various galleries, looking at the French impressionists and, briefly, cubists and whatever the hell Jackson Pollock was; but I spent the most time, as I always did, in among the low-country painters like Rembrandt and Vermeer and Frans Hals. Saturday night we drove up to Baltimore and ate crab cakes in Harbor Place. And Sunday we stayed mostly in bed and read newspapers and tested room service.

I left her at work Monday morning. She kissed me goodbye and we both had a sense, I think, of incompleteness, of something left out. As if we stepped to the tune of different drummers. *Jesus Christ.* I shook my head angrily, alone in the car, and stepped to the tune of mine out to National Airport.

I ditched the rental car and took an Eastern flight back

to Boston. At quarter of two I was pulling up in front of an office building on State Street. Before I went into the office building I looked up to the top of State Street where the old South Meeting House stood, soft red brick with, on the second floor, the lion and the unicorn carved and gleaming in gold leaf adorning the building as they had when the Declaration of Independence was read from its balcony and, before it, the street where Crispus Attucks had been shot. It was a little like cleansing the palate. Washington's federal grandeur faded.

I took the elevator to the eleventh floor and walked down the marble wainscotted corridor to the far end, where a frosted glass door had CONTINENTAL CONSULTING CO. lettered on it in gold leaf that had begun to flake. I went in. The same Utrillo prints were on the walls. A perky-looking receptionist with a plaid skirt and a green sweater smiled at me and said, "May I help you?"

"Joe Broz please."

"May I say who's calling?"

I told her. She spoke into the phone. Then she turned to me. Her face serious. Her nose, I noticed, turned up slightly at the end. Her brown hair was cut short and very neatly groomed. Her nail polish was fresh and dark, almost brown.

"May I ask concerning what matter, Mr. Spenser?"

"Gerry," I said. She relayed the message.

The door behind her opened and Vinnie Morris stood in it. His face was blank, but he was looking at me very hard. He jerked his head and I went in. Everything was the same. The room all in white. The big black desk. The wide picture window that looked out over the waterfront. The dark blue rug. But Broz had changed. Ten years had made him old. His hair was white. He seemed smaller. He was still overdressed and immaculate but much of the theatricality had left him. He didn't seem on camera anymore.

Amazing. And here I was as youthful and vigorous as ever.

"What the fuck do you want?" Broz said.

"Ah, Joe," I said. "It's what makes you special, that little spike of real class."

"I asked you a question."

In addition to Vinnie, Ed was there leaning against the padded bar, an open copy of *People* on the bar in front of him. There was another member of the firm sitting in a black leather chair with his feet up on the coffee table. He had longish black hair and a vandyke beard. He had on a pink cashmere sweater that was stretched to a gossamer web around his upper arms and his waist. Fat, but hard fat. A bodybuilder gone bad.

"This is family talk, Joe. You want them around?"

Without taking his eyes off me he said, "Ed, you and Roger wait in the other office."

They went at once, without question or comment. When they were gone Vinnie leaned against the door, his arms folded.

Broz leaned back. His face was tanned and full of lines. He still had a big mouthful of white teeth and he still wore a diamond pinky ring. And his eyes were without humanity. He nodded his head once for me to begin.

"I can put your kid in the pokey, Joe."

Broz made no movement. It was like staring deep into the eyes of a turtle.

"He's selling cocaine. He's involved in sex orgies with

underage children. He's distributing pornographic materials. I know that and I can prove it."

Vinnie was immobile against the door. Broz's eyes were barely open. Nothing moved.

"What I don't know, but I can guess, is how much of this is performed as your agent."

Still nothing moved.

"I say he's not. I say he's out on his own and trying to be a success on his own to impress the old man."

I paused. There was a crystal stillness in the room. Broz seemed to have gone deeper inside his own silence.

"I say he's also blackmailing Meade Alexander with dirty pictures of Mrs. Alexander."

The sky through Broz's picture window was a clean blue, no clouds, some pale winter sunshine. Below and at a distance I could see the curve of the harbor and the shoreline south past Columbia Point.

Broz's voice when he finally spoke seemed barely connected to him; it seemed to ease out of something deep and remote.

"Tell me about it," he said.

I told him about the death threats to Alexander. I told him about the two kids that got shoved around in Springfield. I told him about Louis Nolan. I told him about the blackmail threat and about the films. I told him that one of the actors in Mrs. Alexander's film was Gerry. I told him about burglarizing Gerry's apartment. About the two teenyboppers, and the cocaine delivery route and the granny party and the talk I had with Bobby Browne in his office with the fake mahogany paneling. Throughout the whole recitation Joe's eyes were barely visible through the lowered slits of his eyelids. He might have been made of terra cotta as he sat tanned, old, and impeccable, without even the signs of breath stirring him. Behind me, at the door, Vinnie was no different.

Then I was through. Broz's gaze stayed on me and then moved away and settled on Vinnie. Only his eyes moved. The tanned, wrinkled face and gray head remained stationary. His old man's hands rested stilly on the desk before him. The pallid sun shining in through the picture window made a small spectrum on his desktop, where it shined through the diamond on his finger.

When Broz spoke it was again in that distant deep remote voice.

"Vinnie?"

"Yeah, Joe. I knew about it."

"And I didn't," Broz said.

"I knew about it after the kid was into it, Joe. I did the best I could."

I looked back at Vinnie. He was as he had been, arms folded, leaning against the door. He paid no attention to me. His eyes were on Broz.

Again silence. I could hear the sound of Joe's breathing now, soft and unlabored.

"And what he's telling me is so?" Broz said.

"Yeah, it is, Joe. Kid wants you to respect him. He . . ." Vinnie shrugged and turned his palms up.

Broz's voice got softer. "I love him," he said. "He should settle for that."

"He ain't very old, Joe," Vinnie said.

Broz nodded slowly. It was the first movement he'd made since I started talking. "I know."

Vinnie was quiet. Broz shifted his look to me.

"You don't have kids," he said.

"Not exactly."

"I didn't either until I was old. What the kid did he did on his own. Some of what he done ain't my way. Dirty movies, that stuff. I don't like that."

"And you don't like him risking Browne on something like this."

Broz nodded. "I invested in him his first time out for office," Broz said. "I been putting money in every year since, investing. Browne gets his cover blown and I've lost money on my investment. You should have told me, Vinnie."

"Maybe. But I knew how you'd feel about it, Joe. I tried to clean it up before you knew."

"My kid, Vinnie, my problem."

"I'd have cleaned it up if Alexander hadn't gotten him." Vinnie pointed at me with his chin.

Broz nodded. "Okay, Vinnie, I was you I'd have done the same." He looked at me. "What do you want?"

"I want the tapes of Mrs. Alexander destroyed. I want the both of them left alone."

"That's all?"

"Yes."

"What about the election?"

I grinned. "May the best man win," I said.

"We could drop you in the harbor," Broz said.

I nodded.

"We'll be in touch," Broz said.

Chapter 28

At 6:45 that evening I was hanging around the shuttle terminal at Eastern Airlines waiting for Paul Giacomin to arrive from New York for the Christmas holidays. Traffic was heavy and the flight would be late.

I stared out the windows at the airport and thought about Joe Broz. He had two roads he could follow. He could kill me and hope I hadn't given evidence on his kid to anyone else. Or he could go along, give me back the tapes, and trust me to keep my end of the bargain. Killing me was the way Joe would normally go. I was hoping this once he'd take the road less traveled. And he might. His kid was involved. He didn't know what I'd done with the evidence, or how much evidence I had, or who else I'd told. He might figure that he could always kill me and wait to see what happened. No way to know really, and since you prepare for what the enemy can do, not what he might, I had my normal .38 under my coat, and a back-up .25 in an ankle holster. I also looked around a lot.

At 7:20 Paul walked up the corridor carrying a suitcase

in one hand and a dance bag on a strap over his shoulder. A young woman came with him. Her hair was pale blond and straight and almost to her waist. Paul had told me about her. Her name was Paige Cartwright. She had a suitcase too. Paul introduced us.

She said, "Mr. Spenser. I've been dying to meet you."

"Paul's been telling you all the funny things I say and do."

"He's told me all about you," she said.

I nodded. "It's not enough you gotta go to Sarah Lawrence," I said to Paul, "you have to carry a purse in public."

He adjusted the shoulder bag. "It's to hold my tutu," he said.

At my apartment we had roast duck with fruit stuffing and three bottles of Pinot Noir and at 1:15 Paul and I sat at my kitchen counter drinking brandy with soda. Paige had succumbed to the wine and gone to bed.

"You've been to see Susan?" Paul said.

"Yes."

"How is it?"

"It's okay," I said. "A little out of sync maybe."

Paul nodded. "She coming home for Christmas?"

"I don't know," I said. "We didn't discuss it."

"You could go down there."

"Sure," I said.

"Paige and I would be fine here. If you want to go down, it's okay."

I nodded.

"You ever think about dating someone else?" Paul said.

I drank some brandy and soda. "Someone else?"

"Sure. That girl you used to go with before Susan. Brenda? You could go out with her."

There were three ice cubes in my glass, and a shot of brandy and the rest soda, except I had drunk half of it. Part of the top ice cube was above the surface.

"No," I said.

"Why not?"

"I love Susan," I said. "I want to be with her. Other people bore me."

"Never, no one but Susan? You never met anyone else?"

"I liked a woman in L.A. Slept with her once."

"Why don't you go visit her?"

"She's dead," I said.

Paul was silent for a moment. Then he nodded. "That one," he said.

"Yes."

The dishwasher finished its cycle and clicked off. The silence was nearly obtrusive in the aftermath.

"It's more than that, Paul. It's more than finding no one else so interesting."

He nodded. "If you could love somebody else, then what would it say about this great love you've been loving for ten years?"

"The new religion calls all in doubt," I said.

"You pay a very high price, as I said last time, for being what you are."

I nodded.

"It makes you better than other men," Paul said. "If you hadn't been what you are, where would I be? But it also traps you. Machismo's captive. Honor, commitment, absolute fidelity, the whole myth."

"Love," I said. "Love's in there."

"Of course it is, and, if need be, to love pure and chaste from afar. But, damn it, I'd like to see you get more back."

"Me too," I said.

"I don't mean from Susan. I mean from life, for cris-sake. You deserve it. You deserve everything you want. You have a right to it."

I drank the rest of my drink and made another one.

"I am what I am, kid. Not by accident. By effort, a brick at a time. I knew what I wanted to be and I finally am. I won't go back."

"I know," Paul said. "You can't even talk about things like this unless you're drinking."

"I can," I said. "But unless I'm drinking, talking about things like this seems pointless. I can't be what I am and love Susan differently."

"And you won't be something else?" he said.

"I worked too hard to be this," I said.

Paul got up and made himself another drink.

"Maybe the question is can you be what you are if Susan's change of life is permanent," he said.

"The way I feel about her won't change," I said.

"How about the way you feel about yourself?"

"I'm working on that," I said.

Chapter 29

Paul slept in my bed with Paige. I took the couch. In the morning I got up with a half hangover and an odd sense that somewhere last night I had turned a corner. I looked at my watch. 6:20. A few miles along the Charles and maybe the half hangover would go away.

I went silently into my bedroom, got my running things, and brought them out to the living room, where I dressed. Running with a gun on the hip is jouncy. But running without one when Joe Broz had speculated about dropping you in the harbor is shortsighted. My solution was to take the little .25 automatic that I used for a back-up. I pumped a shell up into the chamber and then eased the hammer back down and carried it in my hand. It was small enough so that my hand concealed it and other joggers would be unlikely to overreact.

The weather was superior for Boston in December. The temperature was nearly forty and the walkways along the esplanade were clear and black. I began to run along the iver, westbound. To my left the backs of Beacon Street apartments faced out onto the river. A lot of small balconies, a lot of big picture windows, at ground level, and a narrow alley cleverly named Back Street, with parking spaces and occasional garages. Between me and Back Street Storrow Drive was still nearly empty in the slowly developing light. In an hour commuter traffic would fill it, and the air would be thick with hydrocarbons. An MDC police cruiser moved slowly up behind me on the pathway. I stepped aside to let it pass and it drove slowly on and disappeared as the pathway curved with the river.

Paul understood me in a way that few people did. He was only eighteen but he'd had to rebuild from scratch and understood self-creation. He'd explained to me once about how a dancer has to be physically centered in order to perform properly. He was centered in ways beyond dancing and I understood the effort that had gone into it. Some of the effort had been mine. But I hadn't done it. He had done it.

Ahead of me a man in a beige jogging suit unhooked the leash from a golden retriever and the dog dashed toward the river bank, its nose to the ground. Maybe I should get a dog. Man's best friend.

I was feeling pretty good. It was always easier to feel good when something I was working on was winding up. There was a sense of completion. Especially if the windup was orderly. The sun was up now, not very high, but fully above the horizon, and I squinted against it. I hated running in winter. In spring you worked up a good sweat and the muscles rocked easy in vernal heat. But when I didn't run I began to feel angular and stiff, as if I would make a clanking sound when I moved. Runner's high, where are you when I need you?

The way I felt about Susan was not Susan's problem of course. I loved her not for her sake, but for mine. Loving her was easy, maybe even irresistible. It was also necessary, but it was my necessity, not hers. What the hell was she doing so bad? Devoting a lot of time to her work being caught up in it even. So what, thousands of people cared deeply for their work and were able to love one another. Whether I came first with Susan, or second, I could love her as much as I cared to, or needed to. The trick was to do it with dignity. As I went under the Mass Ave bridge I saw a pale blue Buick sedan parked there and standing beside it were Ed and his fat friend with the vandyke beard. Ed pointed a gun at me. So did Vandyke. With my hands at my side I thumbed back the hammer on the .25.

"Joe wants you wasted," Ed said.

I shot him in the chest with the .25 and he spun half around and fell on his side. I hit the ground with him. Vandyke shot at me and hit me in the top of my left thigh and I fired three more shots at him. One of them caught him under the right eye and he was probably dead by the time he hit. I rolled over and checked Ed. He was dead too. I looked down at my left leg. The dark blue cotton sweat pants were black with blood. I undid them and looked at the wound. The bullet had entered on the inside of my thigh and gone right through. It didn't hurt much yet, but it would. I put the gun into the pocket of my jacket, stripped off the jacket, took off the white T-shirt I wore underneath, folded it the long way, and wrapped it around my thigh. I held it there with one hand while I pulled Ed's belt off and strapped it tight around the T-shirt. Then I put on my jacket and pulled up my sweat pants and experimented with standing up. I could. The bone in my thigh was probably not broken. The traffic on Storrow was starting to build, but the chances of flagging someone down were slim. The guy with the golden retriever was nowhere in sight. Neither was the dog. Neither was the MDC cruiser that had passed me earlier. Never a cop around when you need him.

My leg still didn't hurt much, but I felt dizzy and sick. Mass General Hospital was a mile or so back. I swayed a little and looked at the Buick. I took a step toward it and almost fell. I steadied, took a sort of hop, and got my hands on its hood. The motor was running. Balancing against it, I edged along past the two dead men and got in. It was an automatic. A clutch would have been difficult. I put the car in gear, took off the emergency, and drove forward; the car bumped over something that I knew was Ed. But I didn't have much strength for maneuvering. Ed wouldn't care.

It was like driving drunk. I could barely keep my eyes open. With both hands on the wheel I stared as hard as I could at the curving black ribbon of the pathway. Back eastbound I went. I didn't dare go fast for fear I'd lose control. The car wavered as I drove. My head kept drooping and jerking back up as I caught myself. A couple of joggers moved out of my way. They probably glared at me, but I didn't have the strength to notice. All of what I had left channeled onto the asphalt ahead of me. Dimly I realized that the radio was on and a morning man was talking brightly about the last record and introducing the traffic reporter. *Avoid the esplanade; there's a double homicide and a slow-moving vehicle on the footpath.*

The pathway began to waver and the steering wheel got more and more limber. The pathway curved in close to Storrow Drive and the wrought iron fence that separated me from Storrow Drive suddenly surged up in front of me and rammed into the car. The impact made no sound, and as I spiraled down into the dark I could hear clearly the radio still playing: "This is radio eighty-five . . . eighty-five . . . eighty-five . . ."

And I woke up with Martin Quirk leaning over the end of the bed with his hands clasped and his forearms resting on the footboard.

Chapter 30

Quirk said, "The emergency room people tell me you're not going to die."

"Heartening," I said. My voice seemed a little uncoordinated.

"They say you can probably go home tomorrow," Quirk said.

"I'm going home today." My voice was better. I could feel a connection with it.

Quirk shrugged. An I.V. unit was plugged into the back of my left hand.

"Want to tell me about it?" Quirk said.

"I don't think so," I said.

A small blond-haired nurse with big blue eyes came in and took my pulse.

"Nice to see you awake," she said.

"Nice to be awake," I said. Polite.

She smiled and took my temperature. It was one of those electronic thermometers connected to a small pack on her belt. You didn't even have to shake it down. Where was the fun in that? Quirk was quiet while she took her readings. She noted her results on a small chart and said, "Good."

When she was gone Quirk said, "Up under the Mass Ave bridge there are two stiffs shot to death with a small-caliber automatic; four ejected shells are scattered around them. In your jacket pocket the MDC cops found a twenty-five-caliber automatic with four rounds gone. One of the stiffs is Eddie DiBenardi. The car you rammed into the fence is registered to him. The other guy is Roger Francona. He had a nine-millimeter Smith & Wesson with a round missing. You have a hole in your leg. They told me downstairs that you're lucky, it missed the bone. Eddie DiBenardi's belt is missing, and one about the right size was wrapped around your leg when they brought you in." Quirk had straightened and walked to the window and was looking out with his hands in his hip pockets. He turned to look at me.

"Some of us are beginning to suspect a connection," he said.

"You suspect me on that kind of flimsy evidence?" I said.

"Sort of."

I nodded. "They jumped me. They didn't say why. I was jogging along, minding my own business."

"Carrying a loaded gun?" Quirk said.

"Carrying a loaded gun, and these two guys attempted to shoot me."

"And succeeded," Quirk said.

"And I returned fire in self-defense," I said.

"You know either one of them?"

"No."

"Eddie is with Joe Broz. . . . Was." Quirk said. "Roger, we don't know yet. We're still looking into him."

I nodded.

"And, small world, you were just recently sitting in my office reading the OCU file on Joe Broz."

I nodded.

"You care to comment on that?" Quirk said.

"No," I said. My leg felt hot and sore. I felt it with my right hand. It was heavily bandaged. The more I woke up, the sorer it felt. Maybe I would wait till tomorrow to go home. Quirk walked across the room and closed the door.

"How come I'm in a private room?" I said.

Quirk pointed at his own chest.

"I tried to get hold of Susan," Quirk said. "But she's not around."

"She's in Washington," I said.

Quirk rested his butt on the windowsill, folded his arms, and looked at me.

"Okay," he said. "Here's what I think. I think you were bothering Joe Broz and he sent Eddie and Roger out to kill you and they weren't quick enough. If two guys had to go down, they're not a bad choice. I don't know Roger, but I know Eddie. Eddie was a scumbag. I'm willing to bet Roger was pretty much the same. A day in which you shoot a scumbag like Eddie DiBernardi is a day well spent."

"Makes a nice hobby," I said.

"On the other hand," Quirk said, "I am not employed by the city to go around saying 'Way to go' when somebody blows up a couple of citizens in a public park. Even if the citizens are scumbags."

I nodded.

"You see my position," Quirk said.

I nodded some more.

"When you put your mind to it," Quirk said, "you can be an all-world pain in the balls. And you think you're smarter than you are, and you think if you want to do something it must be the right thing to do."

"I'm not as sure of that as I used to be," I said.

"Me either," Quirk said. "But, on the other hand, you haven't done too many things since I've known you that I wouldn't have done if I was you."

"Maybe we're both wrong," I said.

"Probably," Quirk said, "but I don't think there's much we can do about it." He stood up and unfolded his arms and put his hands back into his hip pockets. "Anyway. I don't see a reason to charge you at the moment, but I want some information. Eddie and Roger are not the last two guys that Broz can hire. If he wants you in the ground, he can be persistent. If he succeeds, I want to be able to nail him for it."

"You sentimental bastard," I said.

"Off the record," Quirk said, "what the fuck is going on?"

I told him. All of it.

When I got through Quirk said, "The guy's wife isn't worth it."

"Ronni Alexander?" I shrugged. "She's worth it to Meade."

"Meade ain't the one got shot in the leg," Quirk said.

I didn't say anything.

"You going to keep squeezing Broz?" Quirk said.

"I can't think of anything better," I said.

Quirk nodded. "Okay. I'll do this," he said. "I'll put the word out that I'm, ah, monitoring your well-being on this. It'll get back to Joe. I'll let him know that if you get killed, I'm going to make a mess of his life."

"That'll help," I said.

"Yeah. It will. Joe's very practical. But I don't know. This is family. I don't know if it will help enough."

"Maybe Joe will notice that I'm not easy to hit," I said. "Didn't work out too well this time."

"That was this time," Quirk said. "If he has to, he'll send Vinnie Morris. It's a lot harder to be too quick for Vinnie."

"True," I said.

Quirk got his topcoat from the back of the chair where it lay, neatly folded. "Anyway, that's your problem," he said.

"Also true," I said.

Quirk shrugged into the topcoat. "I called your little buddy down at the Harbor Health Club," Quirk said. "Cimoli. Told him someone had tried to kill you. He said he'd send someone over to comfort you."

"Thanks," I said.

Quirk nodded and opened the door to leave. As he went out, Hawk came in. They passed each other without expression or comment.

Chapter 31

There was a phone in the room and I called my apartment and got Paul and told him I wouldn't be home till tomorrow. I didn't tell him why.

He said he and Paige were going to Quincy Market for the afternoon and that night they were going to see a performance by a dance company I'd never heard of. He said he had enough money and I told him there was no such thing as enough money and we hung up.

Hawk was sitting in the visitor's chair reading a copy of *The Ring* magazine with his feet up on the windowsill. He had removed his down-filled leather jacket and put it on a hanger in the closet. A .357 magnum in a shoulder holster hung under his left arm. He had on a turtleneck sweater, designer jeans, and snakeskin boots.

"Man, you still fighting," Hawk said. "You be rich. They need a great white hope so bad, they'd rank you."

"Maybe it's not too late," I said. "Given what's out there, maybe we could fight for the title."

"You got a plan?" Hawk said.

"To fight for the title?"

"No, to take care of business. Quirk sorta implied to Henry, people might keep trying to shoot you. You got a plan for taking care of that?"

"Why," I said. "You in?"

"Un-huh."

"As soon as I can get out of here I want to see Joe Broz. If we can make it easier for him to go along with me than to kill me, I think we can deal."

"What kind of deal we after?" Hawk said.

I told him, as I had Quirk. All of it. Hawk's face was beaming when I finished.

"Hot diggity," he said. "You actually trying to squeeze Joe Broz? Goddamn."

"What other choice?" I said.

"Tell the congressman to keep his old lady at home," Hawk said. "Or kick her out."

I said, "No."

Hawk grinned.

"I didn't think so," Hawk said. "Just testing to see if your head still soft."

"Quirk says he'll let Broz know that he's interested too."

"Help," Hawk said. "Broz don't want Quirk on his ass."

The same small nurse came in and asked if I was hungry. I said yes and she gave me a meal order menu.

"I'll come back in a little while and pick it up," she said. If she noticed Hawk and his .357, she didn't show it.

Hawk watched her go, his lips pursed. When the door swung shut behind her Hawk said, "Broz probably don't want me and you on his ass either, when you come down to it."

"And I'm betting he doesn't want his kid embarrassed and maybe arrested," I said. "I bet he'll go along."

Hawk shrugged. "We could make sure," he said. "We could kill him. And his kid."

"Have to kill Vinnie Morris too," I said. "Vinnie's like family with Joe."

Hawk shrugged again. "Okay. Joe and the kid, and Vinnie."

"The films might still go public. I don't even know where they are."

Hawk grinned. "She good-looking?"

"Yes."

"Want me to review them? Check for technical accuracy?"

The nurse came back and took my order slip. She still paid Hawk no attention. Must be the training. Hawk was not easy to pay no attention to. Even without the gun under his arm. He weighed 205 and stood six two and had a twenty-nine-inch waist. His skin was densely black and his shaved head gleamed in the hospital fluorescence. When she went away again I said, "The film is accurate."

Hawk shrugged and went back to his magazine.

Lunch came and I shared it with Hawk. After it had digested I got out of bed and tried walking. I could do it with a hobble and a little support from Hawk.

"He ain't heavy," Hawk said. "He's my brother."

"I'll get a cane," I said. "I'll be out of here in the morning."

"Good," Hawk said. "It's awful boring in here."

"No need for you to stay," I said.

"I let you get scragged while you lying in bed and Henry be laughing at me long as I'm living. You know how the little bastard is."

I nodded. "A ball buster," I said.

"Rather sleep in a chair all night than let the little bastard have something like that on me."

"You're right," I said. "I hadn't thought of that."

"Susan be annoyed too," he said.

"I hope so," I said.

Chapter 32

We were meeting Broz on the small footbridge that spans the swan boat lagoon in the Public Garden. I hadn't talked to Broz. I had talked to Vinnie Morris who talked to Broz. When he called back, Vinnie had no comment.

"We'll be there," he said. And hung up.

Hawk drove me there in his Jaguar sedan with a James Brown tape playing loud enough to distract me from how sore my leg was. He parked on Arlington Street in a tow zone and we got out. It was 8:15, not very cold, but dark. I was wearing my other gun on my belt, and had a handful of spare cartridges in my righthand pants pocket. My coat was open.

Hawk went around and opened the trunk and took out a .12 gauge Ithaca pump gun and held it, muzzle down, beside his leg. He shook his head, put it back in the trunk, and took out a shorter gun, double barreled, and tried that out for size. He liked it, nodded to himself, took a handful of shells from a box, and put them into the pocket of his leather jacket. Then he broke open the shotgun, took two more shells from the box, and loaded the gun and closed it. He shut the trunk and with the shotgun, not especially conspicuous, held against his right leg he came around beside me and we walked into the Public Garden. Or Hawk did. I hobbled with my cane. I had traded the aluminum number in for a blackthorn walking stick that Susan had once given me when she thought it would make sense to maximize my Irish heritage with tweed walking hats and paisley scarfs and things. I had tried the hat on once and thrown it and the scarf away. But I kind of liked the stick. One of my ancestors would probably have called it a shillelagh.

There weren't many people in the Public Garden on a December night, but some walked through, and at least two glanced with some uneasiness at Hawk's shotgun. Nobody stopped. We got to the bridge first and there was no sign of Broz. I leaned against the railing in the middle and Hawk moved off quietly for a brief tour of the area. He was back in five minutes.

"Nobody hiding with a rifle," he said. "Nobody under the bridge." I nodded. Hawk drifted down to the end of the bridge toward Charles Street and, with the shotgun hanging at his side, leaned against the little pillars that anchored the bridge. He stayed there, motionless. We waited maybe ten minutes. A tall, thin guy wearing sunglasses and a gray overcoat with a velvet collar walked along the footpath from Arlington Street and onto the bridge. He had his hands in his coat pockets.

"You Spenser?" he said.

"Yes."

"The guy at the end of the bridge, he with you?"

"Yes."

"Who is he?"

"Jiminy Cricket," I said. "He hangs around to make sure my nose doesn't grow."

The thin man nodded. "Wait here," he said.

He walked down the bridge past Hawk and on along the footpath a ways, his head turning carefully as he looked on both sides. Then he turned and followed the footpath back and underneath the bridge and came back on the other side. He came back up on the bridge and leaned against the pillar at the Arlington Street end. In maybe a minute Vinnie Morris appeared and spoke to him. The thin man gestured with his head toward Hawk at the other end of the little bridge. Vinnie nodded and walked away. Two more minutes passed. Then Vinnie appeared with Joe Broz beside him. They walked out onto the bridge and stood beside me. Broz on the side away from Hawk. Vinnie between him and Hawk, in front of me.

Broz said, "What'd you bring the nigger for?"

"I put two of your people in the ground, Joe. Hawk's hoping I'll do it again so he can watch."

"Next time I'll come," Vinnie said.

I shook my head. "No next time, Vinnie. Joe's going to deal."

Vinnie started to speak and Broz said, "Vinnie."

We were all quiet. Hawk motionless at one end of the bridge, the thin guy at the other. Me leaning on the rail. Vinnie looking a little taut in front of me. Broz looking at my face like he was trying to memorize it.

"What's changed?" Broz said. "Why should I deal?"

"For one thing, when you tried to burn me and missed, it got the cops into it. Marty Quirk. You know him?"

"I know Quirk."

"I hear he's taking a special interest in this case."

Broz shook his head impatiently. "Fuck Quirk," he said. "What else?"

"I've had time to make arrangements. Anything happens to me the whole story on your kid goes to the cops and the papers. Pictures, names, everything. And if nothing happens to me, I'm going to stay on the kid's ass until I get the tapes back and Alexander's out from under."

"What else?"

"You didn't need to try and scare Alexander off. He's not going to get elected. He's a joke. He can get elected in his district, but he can't win a statewide election here. When he talks about crime in the streets he means tight pants on women."

"Don't tell me what I know. What have you got?"

"I leave Browne in place," I said. "He's in your pocket, but somebody always will be. He gets elected. You tell him what to do. Alexander goes home to Fitchburg and gets into bible study."

"Anything else?" Broz said.

"No," I said. "That's the package. One way you got aggravation, profit loss, embarrassment, cops in your hair. The other way you don't lose anything. You don't want Alexander anyway."

All of us were quiet. There was no wind. The moon was out. And the stars. Nobody crossed the footbridge. The occasional stroller who approached it detoured when he saw us.

"Okay," Broz said.

Vinnie snapped his head around and looked at Broz. "Joe," he said.

Broz shook his head. "No, Vinnie. I'm going to deal."

Vinnie was quiet.

Broz kept looking at me. "You know why I'm going to deal?"

"My charisma," I said.

"Because of the kid. I'm responsible for the kid. For how he acts. You unnerstand? Joe Broz's kid is supposed to know how to act."

I was quiet.

"He's not just some fucking college boy. He's Joe Broz's kid." Broz shook his head. "He's done this on his own. The whole thing, the coke trade, the videotapes, the two assholes in Springfield. Vinnie got them for him. I don't blame Vinnie. Vinnie was trying to cover for the kid, trying to . . . never mind. I know why Vinnie done it. But things were done using my name and I didn't know about it. And it was stupid." He shook his head again. And stared at me some more. Nobody else said anything. "First time you come around and told me this I was mad. I didn't get to be Joe Broz by letting some punk like you squeeze me. I told Ed to hit you. Vinnie said no. He said Ed wasn't good enough and it was a bad idea anyway. But I was mad, you unnerstand. You was trying to squeeze Joe Broz. You were fucking with Joe Broz's kid."

The traffic sounds from Boylston Street were clear in the silence. On the path that circled the lagoon a couple was walking with a German short-haired pointer on a leash.

"Okay. If Ed had done it right, maybe it would have worked. But he didn't. So you got a deal. But not because you squeezed. You unnerstand that? Not because you squeezed Joe Broz. Because . . . because my kid was wrong."

"And now it's even," I said.

"Yeah. . . . Vinnie, go to the car and get the tape."

Chapter 33

It was Christmas Eve. Susan lay beside me in her bed at her house in Smithfield. Paul was in the living room with Paige watching *Singin' in the Rain* on the late late movie.

"Won't Paige's mother and father be mad that she's not home for Christmas?" Susan said.

"They'll drive down tomorrow for Christmas dinner," I said.

"Gee," Susan said. "An empty nest."

"I'll think of something to pass the empty hours," I said.

"Will I like it?"

"Ecstasy," I said.

"Gee, is Bloomingdale's open on Christmas?" Susan said.

"That's not what I meant."

"Oh." Susan was reading a book called *The Road Less Traveled*. She had closed it on her index finger to hold the place. I was reading a review of the Gail Conrad Dance Company by Arlene Croce in *The New Yorker*. I was trying to learn about dance. I returned to it. The room was quiet.

I glanced at Susan. She still held her book on her lap, leaning back against the sit-up pillow, looking at me.

"A good Christmas for the Alexanders," she said.

"Maybe," I said.

"And she never knew?"

"Nope. She doesn't know anything about what he knows."

"That's insane," Susan said. "He's got to deal with her. He can't just go on waiting for her to do it again. Wondering what she's doing when she's not with him. That's crazy; he can't do it."

"Yes he can," I said.

"For the rest of his life?"

"Until she does something that makes the papers." I put my magazine down and turned a little on my side toward Susan.

"And then what?" she said.

"Then he drops out of public life, if he hasn't already. And tries to put it back together."

"He doesn't leave her?"

I shook my head.

"How can you be so sure?"

"He won't," I said.

"He should. Or he should find professional help. For both of them."

I nodded.

We were both quiet with our book and our magazine in abeyance.

"How are you?" Susan said. I knew she didn't mean my leg.

"I'm all right," I said.

"And how are you feeling about me?"

"Pretty good," I said.

"Better than you did?"

"Yes."

We were quiet again.

"The thing is," I said, "that to be what I am, I need to feel the way I do about you. No matter how you feel about me."

"I feel good about you," she said. "I do love you, you know."

"Yeah. But even if you didn't. The way I feel about you is my problem, not yours. And it's absolute. It can't be compromised. It could exist without you."

"Dead or alive," Susan said. In her face was that quality of serious amusement that so often invested her.

"Probably," I said.

"I wonder what you'd be like as an adult," Susan said.

"I'm post-pubescent," I said. "I can prove that."

"Even with a bullet wound?"

"Sure," I said. "It's almost healed."

Susan dog-eared the page in her book and put it on the nightstand beside her.

"Show me," she said, and edged over beside me and closed her eyes.

Later, early Christmas morning, I was still awake, and Susan was asleep, on her back, with her mouth open slightly. I looked at her face. Her eyes moved slightly behind her eyelids. I watched her sleep; watched her while she dreamed in some remote incorporeal place away from me; watched her with the growing certainty that some of her would always be remote, away from me, unknowable, unobtainable, never mine. Watched her and thought these things and knew, as I could know nothing else so surely, that it didn't matter.